FUR FOX'S
SAKE

ALSO BY MILLY TAIDEN

Sassy Ever After Series

Scent of a Mate *Book 1*
A Mate's Bite *Book 2*
Unexpectedly Mated *Book 3*
A Sassy Wedding *Short 3.7*
The Mate Challenge *Book 4*
Sassy in Diapers *Short 4.3*
Fighting for Her Mate *Book 5*
A Fang in the Sass *Book 6*
Also check out the *Sassy Ever After Kindle World* on Amazon

Shifters Undercover

Bearly in Control *Book 1*
Fur Fox's Sake *Book 2*

Federal Paranormal Unit

Wolf Protector *Book 1*
Dangerous Protector *Book 2*
Unwanted Protector *Book 3*

Black Meadow Pack

Sharp Change *Book 1*
Caged Heat *Book 2*

Paranormal Dating Agency

Twice the Growl *Book 1*
Geek Bearing Gifts *Book 2*
The Purrfect Match *Book 3*
Curves 'Em Right *Book 4*
Tall, Dark and Panther *Book 5*
The Alion King *Book 6*
There's Snow Escape *Book 7*
Scaling Her Dragon *Book 8*
In the Roar *Book 9*
Scrooge Me Hard *Book 9.5 (not full-length)*
Bearfoot and Pregnant *Book 10*
All Kitten Aside *Book 11*
Oh My Roared *Book 12*

Raging Falls

Miss Taken *Book 1*
Miss Matched *Book 2*
Miss Behaved *Book 3*

Contemporary Works

Lucky Chase
Their Second Chance
Club Duo Boxed Set
A Hero's Pride
A Hero Scarred
Wounded Soldiers Set

FUR FOX'S SAKE

Shifter Undercover, Book Two

MILLY TAIDEN

Montlake
Romance

Published by Montlake Romance, Seattle

www.apub.com

Amazon, the Amazon logo, and Montlake Romance are trademarks of Amazon.com, Inc., or its affiliates.

ISBN-13: 9781477848623
ISBN-10: 1477848622

Cover design by Eileen Carey

Printed in the United States of America

To my family. For believing in me and always having my back.
Tito, Aiden, Julie, Alan, Angie, and Mom. I love you all.

CHAPTER ONE

Fellowship agent Devin Sonder stood in his sweatpants staring out his apartment's kitchen window at the scene in the park next door. The coffee mug in his hand started to burn his fingertips, but he was too intrigued in the police activity to notice. Until his panther pawed at him. *Put down the cup, idiot human.*

He did. "Yeah, yeah. If our mate was out there, you wouldn't notice the pain either."

But she isn't. She doesn't exist.

Devin sighed. He almost believed as his animal did. If a mate for them existed, wouldn't they have met by now? But he still hung on a thread to the words his mother had always said: "She's out there; be patient. Fate will guide you to her. Have faith."

His faith was shattered not too long ago when his stepsister and her son were killed because of him. It was his fault. He wasn't there to protect them and they were too weak. He would never again make that mistake, never again get close enough to love someone only to have them ripped away when he wasn't looking.

He often wondered how he could have a mate if he was never loving anyone again. His panther said if they did find her, they were taking her, weak or not, so he needed to get over it. Devin snorted. They'd see who won when it came to keeping their mate safe. If she existed.

Picking up his coffee mug, he headed to the bedroom to change into pants and sports coat, badge in pocket, before crashing the party in the park. In the short amount of time he'd been in Shedford, Oregon, he'd met a few of the local police and actually liked them.

The small town was almost the polar opposite of Los Angeles. He'd been in the LAPD for so long he'd forgotten there were nice people who cared about others. In LA, most of those kinds of humans either had moved away a long time ago or had been killed. Being undercover in the dregs of society had a tendency to jade even the strongest of shifters. Then to have your family taken and tortured—

He stopped those thoughts in their tracks. That time in his life needed to stay in the past. He wouldn't let it overwhelm him as it had before. This was his new start, his second chance.

He opened his closet door. All his pants were pressed and draped over coordinated hangers on one side while starched white shirts neatly hung from the other side. Black socks, all coupled with one tucked inside another, were stacked in the drawer. The Sock Monster did not live in his dryer.

But he did have one weird habit that constantly baffled him. He liked everything in folded order, except his few tighty-whities. He saw no purpose in folding those since they were yanked out of a drawer just to wear under workout clothes. He was a boxer guy, through and through. But when jogging, his boys appreciated a bit tighter fit since they weren't attached by bungee cords.

Dressed and ready for the world, he had made it halfway through the park when the bright yellow crime-scene tape made its appearance, enclosing a section of the popular jogging trail through the woods.

He smelled Detective Tamara Gibbons, one of the Shedford PD's best. She was smart and pretty, could kick ass, and was his coworker's mate. A grin spread over his face. When Mayer and Gibbons happened to be in the same place at the same time, they always provided such entertainment. Which mostly consisted of Gibbons shooting down every come-on and hit Mayer could throw at her.

She looked up as he walked across the grass. "Good morning, Agent Sonder. What brings you out at this early hour?"

He smiled. There was no anger or defensiveness in her voice. She understood they were team players with different cocaptains, not rivals. One department didn't overrule another; they worked together to share info. Again, so different from LA.

"I saw the commotion from my apartment, and you know, curiosity killed the cat. So, here I am." He grinned.

Gibbons laughed. "Well, don't call your partner in yet. I need to get some work done here before he falls all over me."

Devin understood what she was saying. Russel was a great guy, but his thinking head quickly went from one side of his body to the other when Gibbons was in the area.

"You mind if I nose around?" he asked her.

She chin-popped toward the scene. "Any help would be great. Don't be too shocked when you see the vic. Messy, and going to be high-profile very quickly." He didn't like the sound of that. The CSI team arrived and Gibbons headed for them.

He walked toward the pair of running shoes attached to a prone body partially hidden behind foliage. The foot attire was expensive, but well-worn. A routine jogger. The male's hairy legs were toned and long. Some varicose veins, so the victim wasn't young.

He stopped and took in the smells. Wolf—no, wolves. Two. Plus, human blood. Lots of it. Gunpowder. His sharp shifter eyes studied the scene. The ground dirt and leaves were scattered in clumps, suggesting a struggle, or interaction between the vic and perp, at least.

Stepping around the wild brush blocking the man's face, Devin realized what Gibbons had meant when she said "messy and high-profile." Senator Hayseed, their local political celebrity, lay with his throat ripped out, gun in his hand.

"Oh shit," he grumbled. "This can't be good." With such a well-known victim, media, not to mention other federal agencies, would all want to be in on it. His eyes roamed the ground until they stopped on a deformed-looking wolf several feet away. "What the fuck?" He wasn't even sure what he was looking at; it was that strange.

The animal had the normal four legs and canine snout and tail, but the rest was . . . not right. Earlier he'd smelled two scents. Was the other creature dead? He lifted his nose and looked around. And now that he paid closer attention, he noted the scents weren't exactly right for shifters or wild wolves. Something was going on here.

He followed the scent trail into the woods. After some distance, the smell faded too much for his human nose to find, even with his cat's help. He needed to shift if he wanted to continue. Looking around to make sure no one was coming, he loosened his tie and unbuckled his pants. A moment later, he was traipsing through the woods in his panther form.

The farther it led away, the faster he moved to find the other end. The forested area thinned and opened to a space with primitive camp-sites sparsely populated this time of year. The wolf tracks heading this direction disappeared, but bare human footprints marked the dirt. At the edge of a gravel parking area, the footprints stopped, as if getting into a vehicle, perhaps.

Fuck! Not only were shifters involved, but it was now a homicide. He'd better get back to Gibbons ASAP to warn her to get the unauthorized out of the area.

Goddamn, this was not good. Especially after the problem this past weekend with his female coworker finding a shifter bear with amnesia, and a shifter cat woman involved in a couple of mysterious robberies. The origins of the cat shifter were still a mystery.

Back at the scene, he saw more police had arrived to hold back curious onlookers who decided to rubberneck. "Gibbons," he called out.

The detective turned toward his voice as he hurried to her. "This has shifters all over it, and it's now murder."

Gibbons lowered her head and pinched the bridge of her nose. "Damn. I was hoping for normal animals. Should've known." She glanced up at him. "Would you call your people in? I need to get most of these men out of here before they start asking questions." She rushed away, shouting names and orders.

Devin pulled out his phone and dialed his boss, Director Milkan. The man didn't pick up. They had a meeting in the office in thirty minutes. He'd try calling again, but if worse came to worst, they'd talk at the office. He called the group's veterinarian—the "animal whisperer," as they called her, since she could "talk" to critters on four legs.

"Good morning, Devin. Everything all right?" Charli Avers asked.

"No, not really. We have a dead senator in the park with his throat ripped out, and some strange wolflike creature lying dead next to him. I'm needing your expertise."

"Wolflike creature?"

"Yeah. Never seen anything like it."

"I'm on the way in for the office meeting. Should I come where you are first?"

Devin gave that a thought. "I haven't gotten ahold of Milkan yet. So I'll have Detective Gibbons bag it along with the senator's body for the morgue, and we'll see what the boss wants us to do with it during the meeting."

"That sounds like the best plan. Does Gibbons have the right crew there?"

"She's clearing out those who don't know about us. Their clean-up crew is sweeping the scene right now." He wasn't sure how he should approach this next question, so he'd spit it out and apologize later if needed. "Was Barry accounted for this morning?"

"Yes, Devin." He heard the smile in her voice and breathed a sigh of relief. Last thing he wanted was an angry coworker. If he were in LA, he wouldn't have cared. "My bear was with me all night and this morning with no signs of him leaving."

"Good. One less thing to worry about."

"Agreed," Charli said.

He sighed. "I'll get with Gibbons to secure the scene, then see you at the office shortly." He slipped his phone back into his coat pocket. This was going to be another long weekend.

CHAPTER TWO

Marika Paters leaned her body against the front doors of the Fish and Wildlife Service building. Her petite frame barely nudged the hard-to-open door. She had to put some muscle into it. But with her neon-green sneakers on, she had no problem muscling her way in. The shoes weren't neon green because she was hip and into bright things, but because her home was such a mess, she could never find her white ones.

With a spring in her step, she bounded through the front lobby. "Good morning, Ms. Paters. How are you?" the receptionist said. Marika waved back.

"I'm great! How are you this morning?"

The receptionist raised her mug of coffee. "Just a few more of these and I'll be on your level."

Maybe she was just weird, but she had never understood why people thought she was high on caffeine. Granted, she had a lot of pep, but most shifters did. Especially those with a smaller animal. The big bears and cats took so much energy just to get around, and when they shifted, a couple of thousand calories were burned in the process.

For her, the fox inside was perfect. The girl didn't demand very much, was a happy camper most of the time, and always glad to lend a paw when needed. The critter was sometimes excitable too. Depended what was going on or who was going on. They were always on the lookout for their destined mate.

And it always helped that Marika loved her job. She'd always loved learning things and solving mysteries growing up. How did something work? Why was the sky blue? If she took it apart, could she put it back together without a lot of extra parts lying around? What clues existed that would link a killer to this evidence? The kind of questions a research scientist strove to answer.

Her area of study out of college had dealt with animal DNA and the impact of the environment on animals. That was how she teamed up with Charli. At a conference discussing new and emerging technologies in the science of animal studies, she and Charli attended a roundtable and became instant friends. When Marika was offered a job at the FAWS facility as one of the head scientists, she jumped at the chance to be near her friend.

The two were inseparable outside their work. They were two lone wolves—well, a fox and an animal whisperer—on the prowl looking for fun. As time went by, Charli opened her own vet clinic and worked more than she slept. The need for animal forensics in association with crime scenes rocketed, and when Marika wasn't in the lab searching for evidence and clues, she was testifying in courts around the country.

That led to the need for shifter forensics. FAWS quickly became the go-to place when it came to crimes concerning shifters. Mainly because no other facilities were shifter "friendly." Marika specialized in shifter genetics and studied all she could concerning the transitions from ancient to modern shifters. So it wasn't surprising that she was given a special project she wasn't to discuss with anyone.

Several men, including her boss's boss, asked her to attend a meeting in the conference room. As far as the research and forensics teams were concerned, the conference room was where the reprimands were delivered, as well as the *you're fired* speech. *Nervous* wasn't the word for what she felt walking into the room.

But all turned out well. They didn't tell her very much because they didn't know themselves, but the boxes of files lining the side wall were to be her project until it was done. She was to go through the cryptic data and decipher the meaning to see what, or if, it had to do with creating or breeding shifters. Or other technological beings.

That had shocked the shit out of her for a second. Shifters were *created*. But then she thought about humans. Somewhere down the line they were "created" too. But knowing someone took notes and had a direct hand in her life was awe inspiring. Like God saying, *Marika, you are life. Go forth and prosper, but stay away from the damn tree.*

The boxes contained work from a highly advanced people with technology far beyond what Earth had today. There was no question in her mind that aliens were behind the science. Why those aliens had been on Earth, she had no answer, but she had the reason for the creation: protectors of Earth. The ancient aliens' goal was to create a race of creatures that would be able to communicate with both sides of this planet—the animal side and the human side.

The creatures were to make sure the planet was safe from those who would do it harm or cause a downfall in natural resources. She thought that was noble, but shifters had done much more than that throughout history. Their contributions had helped shape the way the world was today, socially and technologically.

She learned how shifters were bred with trial and error, infusing traits and characteristics directly into the DNA, then letting nature take over to smooth out the rough edges of the combinations.

The first few generations of creatures came out very "raw." The human side and the animal side didn't fuse together well. They were more like two entities in one body, always fighting between which would dominate. If the human won, the creature lived. If the creature was more powerful, the person would be killed. Logic had to overrule animal instinct.

Everything had made sense to her—the processes, the ideals, the technology—until she pulled items from the last three boxes. The work documented there seemed . . . off. Previous data had been presented in a logical, concise manner. Easy to read and follow. The last items were more scrawled fragments of thought. Preparations were listed with no results, and results with no prep. Instead of neat horizontal rows, bits and pieces were all over the page. Some had lines connecting things, some things were crossed or scribbled out.

The data also seemed newer. In fact, English had found its way into a lot of the notes. Words easier to say and spell in English were used instead of the alien language. She was guessing the time gap between boxes six and seven amounted to hundreds of years. Where box six left off, box seven didn't pick up. It was as if in box seven the data was trying to recreate things already done. But maybe not actualized.

If she had to guess, she'd say the last few boxes were created by a madman.

CHAPTER THREE

K lamin stood behind his desk, hands squeezed into fists. So much anger built inside him, he wanted to shred the man before him into pieces, rip his fucking head off, beat him until he was flattened. Instead Klamin looked at him.

"Nex, you had one task—to kill the senator and get out—yet you managed to fuck it up. And now the bastards have one of my creations. Do you understand what this means?"

Since Perry, his bear shifter and second-in-command, had shacked up with the curvy veterinarian, he'd been out of his hands for a week. Klamin was forced to promote another shifter to do the dirty work. A fucking, goddamn stupid fuck who couldn't do anything right. Why was everyone around him so incompetent? No, that wasn't right as much as why were the other people so competent?

The fucking fellowship had a burned-out investigator from LA, ready to kill himself because of things out of his control; a dipshit cop who could only focus on his newly discovered mate; and a human female animal doctor. What kind of screwed-up crew was that? Yet the past week, they'd fucked him up the ass, ruining years of planning.

Klamin leaned over his desk, let out a roar, and with one arm swept everything onto the floor. He remained bent over, huffing. He felt a little better after the tantrum, but still wanted to wring the wolf's neck.

At least the senator was dead. Fucking dickhead should've never tried to pull a fast one. Had the man really thought Klamin wouldn't find out? Thanks to centuries of research and development, he knew everything he needed to know instantly.

He turned back to Nex. "How did the old man manage to kill the other wolf?" Obviously, there was a flaw he had neglected to find. This field test had been a good idea, but the enemy having his weapon was damning.

Nex said, "I don't know. I was too busy ripping the man's throat out to notice."

"Hmmm." Klamin paced. He figured the senator more than likely got off a lucky shot. Fortunately, this idiot was able to finish off the bastard. "Did anyone see you?"

"Not directly," Nex replied. "Afterward, I drove around to the park side and joined others watching the police work. They were all human, except for one. He was with the fellowship, the blond male. When he came out of the forest, I left. I believe he knew there were two shifters at the killing."

"Of course he does, dipshit. He's a shifter and can smell you. Don't leave this bunker unless I tell you to. If he smells you now, you're as good as dead. Now get out of my sight." The shifter stood and left the room.

Klamin continued to pace; he imagined the proverbial angry steam rolling off him. *Relax.* He had to relax before he did something irrational. This plan would not be destroyed because a greedy human asshole thought he was smarter and had more power. He was so close to seeing years of painstaking work come to fruition. He would have his full revenge, and those who denied him would suffer.

Thanks to the bank and armored truck heists, he now had enough American money to sustain his projects until launch. If only the last task at the water facility had been accomplished, life would've been perfect.

Now he needed to come up with a different way to hide such high water consumption. The last thing he needed was someone to notice and come out to investigate who was using enough water to supply an army.

It was a shame he had to waste his cat woman. She was so good at getting in and out of places. He'd have to make another one. That would be something his scientist, Sloan, could get on right away. Shit, he'd have to find Sloan on his own.

Going a week without Perry, his real second-in-command, really put a crimp on things. Klamin never realized how much the bear shifter had taken care of. Thank the gods he had the foresight to "preprogram" the bear with instructions for the armored truck heist. If he hadn't, Perry would've never intercepted the vehicle, and his funds would be short.

What he couldn't understand was how the woman vet continuously broke his mind control over the bear. What power did she have over him? Granted, she was delicious-looking with her abundant curves and quite fuckable ass, but Perry could have any female he wanted in the compound. What made her so damn special?

Even after Klamin had sent another minion to run the vet and Perry off the road, the bear again protected the woman. That fiasco had been close to a total fuckup. But it had worked out well, seeing everyone thought the shifter killed in the accident was the person shooting at the couple earlier. Again, that was something Perry would've handled; instead, he'd had to do it on his own. And failed.

Klamin wondered if the amnesia was the cause or simply another side effect of brain damage from forcing the bear into Perry? One thing was certain. As soon as Perry's memories came back, he would kill the veterinarian, no matter how many times he'd fucked her. The only question was whether Perry would go rogue or return to being a serial killer.

CHAPTER FOUR

Devin hurried up the front steps to the fellowship's office building and pulled open one of the double glass entry doors. He greeted the receptionist with his normal smile and wave on his way to the hall door.

"Oh, Detective Sonder," Sally called from her desk, "Director Milkan is home sick today and asked that you conference-call him when the group is ready to meet."

He paused at the door for her to buzz him through. "Thanks, Sally. We'll do that." Hearing the sound signaling the release of the security latch, Devin opened the door and left the lobby before Sally could say anything else.

He held nothing personal against her, but he smelled her interest in him when she was close. That rubbed his animal the wrong way. She wasn't his mate, so the panther wanted nothing to do with her. Which was fine with him. Sally was cute and all, but he didn't want to get anything started that he'd have to put a stop to. As it was, he hadn't had any female interaction in so long, his cock was sending out SOS messages for him to remember it was there.

Inside the office, he stopped at his cubicle, hung his sports coat on a hanger, and laid his notebook on the completely organized desk, next to a new ivy-like plant. He wondered where it had come from. He liked plants and the fresh oxygen they provided. His cat loved to roam the woods, so being in an uncrowded area filled with forests was a perfect match for them.

He logged in to his computer to go through his e-mail for important messages. Finding nothing that couldn't wait, he stood and saw Russel and Barry standing together at a cubicle.

He wondered about Barry, the bear with amnesia. The man seemed nice and was a true mate to Charli, so he had to be a good guy, right? Not like Devin got a bad vibe from the guy. Even though Barry had lost his memory, Devin knew that when it came to Charli, Barry didn't lie and he loved her. The scent of his feelings filled their office and came off the bear in waves.

After his and Russel's visit to the hospital when Charli was run off the road, Devin didn't know what to think. Neither did his panther. Usually the animal was quick and spot-on when he came to judging others. And with uncertainty came uneasiness.

Clearly *nice* and *love* had nothing to do with not being a thief. Fact was Barry had something to do with stolen items, but the bear claimed to not remember anything beyond a week ago when he woke in Charli's animal clinic.

When they were in the hospital room, he'd smelled no lies from the bear, so he gave him the benefit of the doubt. But there was still a mystery surrounding Charli's mate and how he fit in with the bad guys. Not to mention the fact that none of the stolen loot, money or jewels, had been found yet. And his paws had supposedly been on both at one time or another.

Charli's head popped above her cubicle. "You guys ready to meet?"

"Milkan's sick," Devin said. "We'll call him when we get started. We can use the conference phone in his office." The group filed into the director's space and gathered around the table opposite the desk in the room. Devin dialed their boss.

The first thing they heard after the phone's ringing stopped was a series of sneezes, deep and growly.

"Milkan," Russel started, "you okay, man?"

Another growl came over the line. "Don't ask. Fucking flu." The man sniffled and blew his nose. Charli cringed. Devin was sure she was very conscientious about germs, being a doctor. Which made him wonder why a veterinarian would be included on a policing force. She had some of the basic detective training the local area provided, but had yet to go to Quantico for the real stuff.

He'd heard her say it would be hard to leave her clinic for the duration needed to train. Seemed she was the only farm-animal vet in the area. Anyone who cared enough to stick their entire arm into the backside of a pregnant cow, may the gods bless them. He sure as hell wouldn't be doing that. A slight shudder rippled through him.

He also wanted to see how she used her "whispering" ability. The fact that a human could effectively communicate with animals blew his mind.

"Sorry 'bout that, everyone," Milkan said. "Let's get started. You're all aware of Senator Hayseed's death?" Devin knew Charli was aware since he'd called her, but Russel knowing came as a surprise.

Russel said, "Sally informed me when she heard it from a friend, who heard it from a friend, who—"

"Got it," Milkan said. "Thank you, Mayer."

This would be a good time to fill everyone in on his discoveries. "Sir, the crime scene this morning was close to my apartment and I checked it out before coming into work." He paused for the director to make any comment. He didn't. Did that indicate he was angry?

That was the problem conducting business over the phone or e-mail—his animal couldn't smell the emotions coming off the other person. Without that sensory input, he felt at quite a disadvantage. He continued, not knowing what else to do.

"I scented shifters, wolves." Nobody said a word, but all eyes in the room were on him. "There was a deformed creature that was dead.

16

I trailed the other to the far side of the park where I found footprints that ended at a car parking area."

Charli shifted in her chair. He scented and saw her unease. "Did Gibbons take the dead animal to the morgue?"

"Yes, along with the senator's body," Devin replied. The director still hadn't said anything. Since their group was formed a short time ago, Devin hadn't been able to fully study his coworkers to discover their idiosyncrasies. Maybe this was normal for his boss. "Milkan, you still there?"

"Yes," the boss almost barked. There were nice drunks and mean drunks. Obviously, the director wasn't a nice sick person. Memo to self, *Never get the boss drunk*. "Sorry, Sonder. I'm miserable right now."

"No need to apologize, sir," Devin said. He couldn't remember the last time he was sick. Well, *sick* sick. From a virus, and not his self-inflicted pain. He pushed that line of thought away. "How do you want to handle the case?"

"Sonder, since your cases are mostly closed, you take it. Try to wrap up the robberies so we can move on."

"I'd like to visit the woman in the hospital," Devin said. "You know, from the jewelry heist."

"Chief Charter said she was still out of it. I doubt she could tell us why she was in the water company's database, but go ahead. See what you can find out," Milkan directed. "Let me know if you get anything new."

"I'd really like to know where the money and jewelry are," Devin said. He'd probably keep the files partially open until everything was solved. He hated not having everything closed in a nice, neat package.

"Which brings up the armored truck robbery," Milkan said. "Mayer"—the director sneezed twice, then blew his nose again—"Mayer, I want you to talk with Gibbons at the PD this afternoon about what she's got on it."

Russel nearly popped out of his seat with joy, then gathered himself. "You can count on me, sir." The shifter's voice was deep, and fake, causing Charli to laugh.

The director came back. "I'd give you a warning, Mayer, but I'm fully confident the woman can keep you in line." The others at the table laughed while Russel rolled his eyes.

"Yes, sir."

"Charli, I hear you. Good to have you back. Hope your few days off were relaxing." Her face blushed and the scent of her embarrassment, tinged with sex, filled the air.

"They were. Thank you, sir. Oh, and one thing. You said for me to tell you when I might have a conflict with working," she said.

"I did. What've you got?" the boss asked.

"I have a cow about to go into labor any day. She miscarried previously, and I want to make sure this one goes well."

"Not a problem, Avers. We should limit the amount of responsibility you carry until we get you fully trained in procedures, anyway. Do what you can, and when you have to leave, let me know. How's your shifter's memory? Anything come back yet?"

"No, sir. I—I—" Worry scented from the woman.

"No need to be concerned, Avers. I was just getting caught up with you."

"Yes, sir. Thank you, sir." She breathed easier. And was truthful in her answer. Maybe Devin should ask her if she had any ideas how Barry was related to the robberies. He'd trust her answers, and trust wasn't something he gave out anymore.

"Anyone got anything else that can't wait until I get back? If I come back. I may shoot myself if this gets worse." Everybody shook their heads.

Devin responded, "I think that's it, sir. Stay in bed and drink noodle soup—"

"With stars," Russel tossed in. "They're easier to get down than noodles. Plus the feel of noodles sliding down your throat is like swallowing a sna—"

"Got it, Mayer." The conference phone clicked and silenced. Devin pushed the disconnect button.

Devin ran through the conversation in his head, recalling the things they needed to discuss, if any. "Ah, the cat woman," he started. "Either of you want to see her too?"

Russel replied, "I would. I'd like to see if she can tell us anything about the armored truck before I visit my mate at her office."

Devin grunted. "Better take flowers with you."

"Why?" Russel looked baffled.

"To apologize in advance for all the idiotic things you're going to say while there." Charli snorted a laugh, and he smiled. But Russel remained dead serious.

"Shit, man. You're right. What time at the hospital?"

Devin's plate was definitely full with the new murder investigation on it. But he still wanted to close those two cases from last week. "How about two o'clock? That work?" The others agreed and scattered for their desks.

Once again he saw the plant on his desk. "Who brought the plant in? How'd you know I like ivy?" Charli and Russel looked at each other, then at him.

"Each of us got one too. We thought you brought them in earlier. Neither of us did."

"Wasn't me. This is my first time in the office this morning." He shrugged and set the pot on a neatly organized shelf to catch more light. "Charli, you have time to go to the ME's office with me to look at this wolf thing?"

Charli looked at her phone, then said, "Yeah, now would be a good time."

Devin grabbed his coat. "Mayer, you coming?"

"Sure, man," Russel said. "You got my curiosity piqued. I want to see what a deformed shifter looks like."

CHAPTER FIVE

Devin led his partner and Charli down the hall to the autopsy chamber. Barry came along too. He'd shown up with Charli. Suddenly Charli stopped. "Barry, I think you might want to wait up front for us."

The shifter lowered his brows, apparently not liking the idea of being away from his mate. Which is how it should be, not that Devin would know.

"Why?" Barry asked.

Charli stared at him, making small, strange movements with her head and eyes. "Because it's the *autopsy* room. Remember Marika and the samples?"

The man's face paled. "Oh, got it. Yeah, I'll be up front watching for anything suspicious." He turned and hurried away. That was weird.

Charli looked at Devin. "I'll tell you later. Basically, he's not a blood-and-guts kinda guy. Well, his own blood, anyway."

Devin was so shocked by what Charli revealed, he forgot to keep walking. How could a shifter, part wild animal, not like blood and guts? What did the bear eat when shifted? Filet mignon, well done?

"Wow," Russel said. "That goes against nature, man. Eating dead, bloody animals is up there with sex: you gotta have it or die."

"We don't die without sex," Devin replied.

"Maybe you don't," Russel said, "but I sure as hell would. And I'm about to die soon, come to mention it. Need to get a new fleshlight."

"Flashlight, you mean?" Devin asked. Charli covered her grin with her hand and walked past them.

"No," Russel retorted. "A fleshlight."

"What's that?" Then Devin thought about the context the word "fleshlight" was used in. "On second thought, never mind. I don't want to know."

Russel laughed. "Aww, come on, man. I'll get one for you too." Charli busted out in laughter ahead of them. "What color you want?"

He shook his head. He'd google the meaning later. "No, you sex addict. I don't want one."

Russel slapped him on the arm. "Chicken."

Devin raised a brow at the name-calling. He could play rough too. "Shove it, Mayer."

"Yup," Russel smiled, "that's what you do with it." In full belly guffaws, Charli fell against the wall and slapped it with her hand. He watched her grandiose display of amusement. How did she know about male sex toys, anyway?

With little more delay, the three entered the ME's cold domain.

"Good morning, Agent Sonder." A woman dressed in scrubs had just completed situating the wolf's body as they entered.

"Hi, Dr. Williams. Thank you for helping us pull the animal so quickly," Devin said as he stared at the monstrosity on the steel table before them.

"Not a problem, Agent. I'm curious to find out what disease or whatever this animal has that made it so . . . weird-looking."

Devin gestured to his female companion. "Dr. Williams, this is Charli Avers. She's our forensic veterinarian, you could say. She's here to see what we've got." Charli reached out to shake hands, but Dr. Williams raised her arms into the air, showing off her elbow-length gloves.

The woman smiled. "I'll have to shake your hand later, Ms. Avers."

"Please, call me Charli," Devin's coworker said.

The lady nodded toward a cabinet. "Well, Charli, everything you need is in the cabinet. Gloves and masks are underneath. Will you be digging in?"

Digging in? Devin's stomach turned. Maybe he'd join Barry out front.

"Not right now. We'll just do an external exam here. I will probably have the carcass taken to my clinic so it's out of your way here. When is the senator scheduled?"

"I've been asked to hold off," the examiner said.

"Why?" Devin asked. He wondered who had the authority to make that happen.

She held her arms up again. "I don't know why, and was told I'd know when I needed to know." Disgust rang in her voice. Seemed like someone pulled rank and she wasn't pleased with it.

Charli asked, "Would it be possible to see the wounds inflicted on the senator? That may help with my part of the investigation."

"Sure, come on over here." Dr. Williams led Charli toward a bank of drawers where bodies were held until processed. Yeah, Devin didn't need to see the senator again. Once was enough.

Russel grabbed his arm. "Do I want to see the body?"

He snorted. "If you do, don't throw up on my shoes."

Russel appeared to think about that. "Okay. I'm staying here. Don't want puke breath when seeing my mate later."

Devin almost laughed, thinking Russel probably wouldn't get close enough for her to even notice. Instead, the two stared at the monster on the table. The back of the animal's skull had been blown away. He'd never seen that before and wondered how that could happen.

The creature's face had dark, thick growths completely covering it. Only the eyes and nose holes were free from the lumpy material. He reached out his hand to touch it, and the word *stop* rang in his ears, echoing across the tile- and metal-clad room.

Both women stared at him with warnings in their eyes. He snapped his hand back and cradled it against his chest as if bitten.

"It's not a good idea to touch it with bare hands," Charli said. "You never know what kind of microbes or germs are on the surface." She turned to Dr. Williams. "Thank you for your help. I'll suit up for external checking. Will you be here?"

"I'll be in the other room. I have a lot of things to do before we're overrun with feds and media wanting to know everything about this. Just so you know, I'm labeling this death as an animal attack. That's all the press needs to know."

Devin gave a nod. "Thank you, Dr. Williams." The woman left and Charli headed to the supplies to suit up. Donning a mask, safety glasses, and long gloves, the vet approached the killer.

First thing she did was take a close look at the animal's face. She thumped a finger against it, then a knuckle. "This covering is very dense and quite hard." Her scalpel picked at an edge. "It's also a part of the skin, not a growth like I first assumed. Interesting."

Next she dug her fingers into the wolf's fur, down his neck to the shoulder. "Both you guys put on a pair of gloves and feel this." Devin looked at Russel, who shrugged then went to the cabinet. They came back gloved and ready for whatever. He hoped he wouldn't end up vomiting. He really hated that.

"Here," Charli said, "dig your fingers into the fur and tell me what you think."

Devin slid his hand over the fur, then pushed his fingertips in. The coat was so thick, he couldn't get down to the skin. "I've never felt anything so lush. The fur is jam-packed. I can't even feel the skin."

"Hey," Russel said, "what's this?" He lifted his hand from the fur and came out with a mashed silver bead between his fingers. "Holy shit, it's a bullet. These fuckers are bulletproof."

"That's not possible," Charli said. "Let me see that." Russel handed over the projectile and she held it up to the light. After close scrutiny, she set it on the table in front of Devin. "Take some pictures of that and send them to Detective Gibbons. Then get her on the line for me, please."

Devin glanced at Russel to see his reaction to calling his mate. The multishifter nodded, giving his permission. As he snapped pictures with his phone, Charli continued her inspection, feeling around the growth surrounding the legs, then higher.

"The muscles are much larger than what they should be for a wolf this size."

"Larger, as in how?" he asked.

"As in, if Arnold Schwarzenegger were a wolf, he would look puny compared to this guy. That's why it looks deformed. The muscular system is grossly overgrown." Her hands slid around the body. "With this mass of body weight, its heart, lungs, and circulatory system all have to be larger, stronger to support it."

"So basically," Russel said, "we have a shifter on 'roids."

"Big steroids," she confirmed. Having reached the tail, Charli walked around the table and carefully adjusted the fractured skull in the light. After poking around, she frowned and her brows pulled down.

"What?" Devin asked.

She let out a breath behind her face mask. "It shouldn't be surprising, yet it is. The bone thickness is much greater than it should be. But with the added muscle and fur density, it's what's needed to physically support the animal." She shook her head.

"I've e-mailed the photos to Gibbons," Devin said. "Are you ready to talk to her?" Charli nodded but didn't look at him. Her frown had been a permanent fixture for the past several minutes.

After a couple of rings, the female detective answered. "Where did this bullet come from, Sonder?"

"Good morning to you, Detective Gibbons." He almost laughed at her excitement.

"Yeah, yeah. I already said that a few hours ago." He heard the friendly banter in her voice. "Now, spill. Is this from the critter? Why isn't it bloody? Did it kill the wolf—"

"Whoa," Devin blurted. "I think we have some questions for you first. I'm putting you on speaker with Charli." He laid his phone on the table between the wolf's feet.

"Good morning, Tamara. This is Charli Avers. How are you this lovely morning?"

"Wonderful, as usual. Thanks for asking. Seems your morning is about as boring as mine."

Charli laughed. "Yeah, I'm sure you're more bored than I am, with such a high-profile case going."

Tamara snorted. "It's already started. One of the big news stations from Seattle called wanting an exclusive. How can information possibly get out that quickly and that far? I barely have the file started."

Charli laughed again. "That's social media for ya."

"Yeah, no kidding. So what have we got in these pictures Devin sent?"

Charli ran down the list of things they'd discovered about the strange shifter, including the bullet. "I was hoping your dad could take a look at it and tell us what he thinks before he goes to the lab over the weekend."

"I'll send these to him, but I can give you some insight also. I've done a lot of work with him when I'm not on call," Tamara said.

"Anything is greatly appreciated." Charli straightened, then reached for the projectile.

"It looks like a normal bullet from a .22 handgun, which our victim had on his person at the scene. The front isn't damaged like those that hit solid material, but the sides are crumpled as if impacting something."

Charli nodded. "So how can a bullet have characteristics of both impact and nonimpact?"

"I've actually seen this recreated in the lab. Usually the gun is fired at something like gelatin or tofu, where it impacts softly, but stops with enough force that the back end presses against the front, making the material buckle and overlap like this." Silence came over the line. Devin was about to ask if she was still there when her voice flowed out again.

"Going off what you described, Charli, it appears we have a bullet-resistant animal. Maybe even bulletproof."

Russel joined in the conversation after being unusually quiet. "What's the difference between bullet resistant and bulletproof?"

Devin heard a tiny gasp from Detective Gibbons and a second of silence. He wondered if the icy detective was affected more by her mate than she led everyone to believe. His fellow agent had himself a mind game with his mate, and Devin questioned who'd break first. He hoped he was there to see it.

Gibbons cleared her throat. "One material no bullet can get through, and the other stops lower calibers or lower speeds, but not all bullets. Very few materials are totally resistant. And nothing in nature is that strong, that I know of.

"If the animal has this type of protection, then it's something that could rewrite ballistic physics. My dad would absolutely fall over himself to see this fur."

"I'm sure a lot of scientists would," Charli added.

"So if the wolf is bulletproof, how was its head injured?" Gibbons asked. "Was it bashed in?"

Charli stood over the front of the table. "The bone fragments look like they were blown out. I'd guess the senator pulled off the only stunt that would've been able to kill this animal. The bullet happened to go through the wolf's open mouth and out the back. And unfortunately, there was a second wolf there luckier than the first."

"Yes, unfortunate for the senator," Gibbons said. "Devin said this is a homicide. Still the same?"

"I'd say yes. But who the responsible human is, I don't have a clue." Charli looked at Devin. "Ever had an issue where you needed to see the human side of the shifter locked in animal form?"

"Yeah, but never found a solution for it. The animal stayed an animal after dying."

Charli sighed. "Detective Gibbons, I'll poke around more and see what else I find. I'll let you know if anything significant shows up."

"Thanks, Charli. Talk to you later."

Devin pushed the End Call button on his phone. Charli stepped back and sighed.

"I think I'd have better luck and top-notch equipment if I went another route rather than taking this thing to my lab." She stripped the gloves off and pulled out her phone. She looked at Devin just as Barry walked into the room. "Only one person in the world can help me, and she happens to be fewer than thirty minutes south of here."

CHAPTER SIX

At her office desk at the Fish and Wildlife Service, Marika set her coffee cup on a file that had brown rings from previous mugs. She would've used the cute coaster she received as a birthday gift from Charli, but she couldn't find it on her desk. She knew it was somewhere. Maybe on the table under the loose piles of papers, or maybe on top of the file cabinet under the stack of journals and magazines. She'd find it one day. Yeah, right. Just like she'd find her mate one day, her animal reminded her for the millionth time.

Now that Charli had found her man, Marika wanted hers too. Not to mention her fox went on nonstop about how it was time to put away the microscope and lady toys and find a man who would give them kits. Lots of kits. Marika put the brakes on there. Kits in the plural was fine, but kits as in their own baseball team wasn't in the plans. She'd gone to school and worked hard to get where she was. Did her animal really want to waste all that time?

Yes. Go Team Paters!

No, Mari wasn't going for that. Besides, it wasn't her fault she hadn't found her mate. Her fox disagreed. It had been established the first hour of her first day at the lab that her counterpart was not a fellow employee. The fox was ready to move on then.

But Marika held her ground, telling the animal to chill out. She would go to social events to meet others and keep an eye out for him. But as time went on, and Charli's vet clinic took up more and more of her time, Marika submerged herself in work, seeing less and less of the world outside the lab.

Then a few months ago, she'd been recruited to study data from ancient beings who had come to Earth and supposedly "created" shifters. The story behind it all was fascinating and so unlikely that if she hadn't met a descendant of the beings, she never would've bought into it. But government officials were part of the group to discuss the research, so she figured some of it had to be legit.

This was far more important than birthing a bunch of kits, which anyone could do, as long as they were shifters to begin with. This was creating something from nothing.

Up to about a week ago, that had mollified her fox. But the sudden appearance of the bear shifter Barry, who claimed he wasn't born a shifter, sent everything into a spiral between her and her fox.

Her animal wanted what Charli now had: someone to snuggle with on cold nights and chase through the fresh mountain air and have a family with. Marika wanted to know how Barry, the ideal specimen for her project (probably the only suitable person on the planet), happened to fall into her—rather, Charli's—lap. She'd slept little this past week, examining and comparing Barry's physical characteristics to hers, a naturally born shifter. She couldn't wait for the couple to pop out a cub so she could see what nature would do.

Her cell phone rang. She quickly felt around her buried desk for the device, accidentally jarring the file folder her coffee sat on, knocking over her Styrofoam cup. Marika jumped up looking for something to sop up the liquid before it soaked into all her papers scattered on the desk. Seeing nothing, she whipped her lab coat off and threw it on the desk.

On the second ring, she remembered why she'd knocked her coffee over in the first place and searched her pants pockets for the damn device. Coming up empty on the third ring, she realized the sound came from her lab coat, now soaking up the brown liquid.

She slammed her hands onto the coat, feeling for something hard and rectangular. Fingers touching a solid object, she flipped the coat over and over, trying to find the pocket, flinging cold coffee drops around the desk.

During the fourth ring, she pulled the device from a pocket. Without looking at the call ID, she swiped the screen and icon for a Skype call.

"Hello, I'm here. Don't hang up." She sucked in a gasp of air and heard the tinkle of her best friend's laughter from the tiny speaker and saw her happy face on the small phone screen.

"I know not to expect you to pick up until at least the third ring, Mari," Charli said. Marika grinned. Her friend was right. No matter how hard she tried, she could never keep up with where she stowed the damn phone. "Whatcha doing, girl?"

Marika dropped the lab coat onto the desk. "Not much, just cleaning up spilled coffee."

"Let me guess," Charli said. "Using your lab coat again because you still haven't brought in paper towels like I keep telling you."

Well, dammit. She did keep forgetting to bring a roll. She did keep using her white overcoat. And like best friends, they knew each other inside and out.

"Okay, Ms. Smart Ass, what are you doing? And if the answer's sex, I don't want to hear it. Or your answer." She smiled at her own funny, and her shifter ears picked up noises across the phone line, but she didn't see anyone else onscreen. She'd die laughing if Charli was in a room of shifters and everyone heard her remark through a speaker. She bounced on her toes waiting to see.

Charli choked on the other end. "Oh my god, Marika. I can't believe you just said that." Marika knew it! She burst out laughing and jumping, imagining Charli's red, red face among the group of shifters.

Barry's voice came from the background. "Charli, tell her if we were having sex, a phone call to her would be the last thing on your mind as you're shouting out my name." Marika then heard a slap and subsequent "oww" with laughter from Barry.

With a huff, Charli said, "Okay, do you want to know why I'm calling or not?"

She smiled. "Of course I do. You'd better be inviting me to some food event. I've got some doozies to tell you that I discovered the last few days."

"Really? Great. And I've got a dead wolf in the morgue, the likes of which you've never seen nor will again."

"No way. Did you hit it with your truck and mangle it beyond belief?"

Barry's and others' laughs came through along with another slap. Charli said, "Now, why would you say that?"

Marika rolled her eyes. She couldn't believe Charli would ever forget that night—

"Oh," Charli said. "Don't you say one word about that. I'll so—"

Marika laughed. "I'm not. I know you have extra ears nearby."

"I'm not listening," Barry said. "It's not my ears that are extra."

"Mine, either," came a voice she'd not heard before. Then a man's face leaned in front of Charli, taking up the whole screen. He was drop-dead gorgeous with his perfect hair and dark eyes. And if she was seeing correctly, his eyes morphed into feline, meaning he was a shifter and his animal was close to the surface in response to her.

Her fox dashed up front and center and stuck her nose against her mind like pressing your face against a window to see in better. Marika told her fox to calm down. They were talking on the phone, which had no smell, she reminded her. But the man looked damn fine from her perspective. Man, it had been so long since she'd had sex, but he looked perfect to get her out of her self-induced abstinence.

"Hi," he said. "I'm Devin Sonder." His voice was dreamy and strong. Sent tingles running to her female parts. First time in forever. Holy wow. Her human side hadn't been this interested in a man in a long time. And he wasn't even in the same room.

Her fox pushed at her skin. Obviously, she liked him too. But just because she turned suddenly horny didn't mean he was their mate. It meant she'd take him down anywhere and practice making kits with him. She licked her lips and his eyes flashed purely animal. Oh god. She was going to orgasm on the spot.

He smiled and her undies got drenched. "Do you have a name?"

Oh fuck. How embarrassing. She'd been lost in sex thoughts when she should've been giving her name to him. Man, he really got to her and the wet spot on her panties. Shit. Thank god she was the only shifter in the lab. Devin's brow raised and she realized she still hadn't given him her name.

"Marika!" Her cheeks flushed hot. "Paters. Marika Paters. Uh, nice to meet you, Devin." His face momentarily disappeared and the image blurred between his face and Charli's. Must've been fighting for the phone. The man she'd soon get naked (maybe) won. His smile returned.

"Are you at your office for a little bit? I'd like to meet you," he asked.

Oh yes. She was all for that. "Charli can give you directions. I'll be here, waiting." That didn't sound too desperate, did it?

"I'll see you shortly." His image jerked away and Charli's grinning face appeared before she put the phone on normal mode.

"Is this what I think it is?" Charli asked.

Marika tried to act nonchalant about the whole thing. She shrugged a shoulder. "Eh, maybe." Then excitement bubbled up, too much for her to keep in. "Oh my god, Charli. He is really hot!" Marika jumped up and down in a circle, then froze. "Why didn't you introduce us earlier, Charli? You keeping him from me?" Female shifter jealousy crept up.

Nobody better touch him. She didn't even know why she was suddenly so possessive of a guy she didn't even know.

Charli snorted on the line. "Right, Mari. Like I had a freaking clue you two would react that way to just a phone call." She could practically hear her friend roll her eyes. "Now, do you want me to show you this animal or not?"

"Yes, Charli, bring me this amazing dead wolf, and I'll share with you two what I've got. I'll give you a little teaser. As far as the world's concerned, Barry doesn't exist."

CHAPTER SEVEN

Devin took his foot off the gas pedal as he realized he was going a little over the speed limit—about twenty miles per hour over. Shit. How would it look for a former police officer to get a speeding ticket? If the ticketing officer was a shifter, he'd understand the rush; if not, then Devin was screwed.

Screw—yes, please. His animal's first thoughts went straight to the gutter. He'd better pull his mind out of there. He was not screwing this gorgeous woman that pulled at his animal's desires (and every dirty human one) within the first minutes of meeting. How barbaric. His panther disagreed. But he was an animal; what did Devin expect?

Devin let out a sigh and thought back to hearing her voice for the first time. He'd never heard anything so melodious in his life. And her laugh sent joy through him, something he hadn't felt for a long time.

Then seeing her beautiful face on Charli's small phone . . . his heart melted. The fact that his chest constricted and the word *mate* floated in his mind made him extra nervous. Could she be? Mate. He'd never heard of anyone recognizing a mate via a video call. Maybe he was just really fucking horny. *Or maybe she really is your mate, you dumbass.* In his dreams, she wasn't nearly as stunning as real life.

Could his luck finally be turning around? He'd believed for so long that his mate didn't exist. That he didn't deserve love because of what happened. Maybe he was wrong.

But he knew he couldn't spend much time with her. He had the damn murder investigation to start. The first forty-eight hours were crucial when it came to crimes such as this and finding the perp. After those initial few hours, odds of catching the killer dropped drastically. The FBI wouldn't let the murder of a senator go unsolved, even if they had to find an innocent body to take the fall.

If it came to that, he'd wash his hands of the case. If it wasn't by the book, he didn't want any part of it. He'd learned his lesson well. Strict adherence to rules and codes was the only thing that mattered. Well, maybe with his mate, he might bend those rules just a bit. Or a lot. He cringed at the thought. Should he press his luck like that? Absolutely not.

He would allow nothing to hurt his mate. He would guard her night and day, twenty-four seven. Occasionally, she could go to the bathroom by herself, if he felt confident she was safe. No one would take her away from him. The dark side of humanity and shifterkind had been imprinted on his soul. More than enough murders, blood, and deaths rested in his tortured mind.

He slowed for the turn Charli described when giving him directions to the Fish and Wildlife Service. Pulling into the parking lot, he saw a woman pacing along the side of the building. That was her. He knew it was. His panther almost leaped forward.

Marika felt so dumb. *I'll be here, waiting*, she'd told him. Like she was dangling on his every breath. Even though she was, he didn't need to know. What if he wasn't her mate? She'd just made a fool of herself. Did she sound desperate? Oh god, she did. Her office was a mess. She headed outside to wait for him. Maybe the fresh air would chill her out a little.

Leaning against the building, she was less chilled than when she walked out. Her fox reacted to the outdoors and spazzed, happy to be in the sun and waiting on the man that could possibly be their mate. *Maybe*, she reminded. Yeah, her fox was sure this was him. If not, she'd kick his ass for getting her hopes up.

Maybe they could have lunch together. Shit. She had promised her mother she'd come over for lunch today. Her mom was cooking one of her favorites—lasagna. Would it be okay to invite him? Would it be too soon to meet her mom? But if he were her mate, they'd mate and do the marriage thing anyway, right? Why put it off, then? Her fox wholeheartedly agreed. Whatever. If her mate said jump off a bridge, her fox would agree. *Maybe.*

On the street out front, a car slowed and turned in. Could that be him? She glanced at her watch. That was record time. She'd never made it that quickly from Shedford before. With a breath out, she tried to remain calm and look as normal as she could standing beside a building ogling the street.

Before she realized she was moving, her fox had pushed her down the sidewalk toward the parked car in front of the main door. He was getting ready to step out. Her first full glimpse of the man she might spend the rest of her life with. Her heart fluttered. She prayed she wouldn't pass out from the excitement.

As she stepped off the sidewalk next to him, he straightened and turned. In his hand was a narrow square box. Her presence must have startled him since he jumped back with wide eyes. Then he said, "Did you order the pizza? It's twelve dollars and fifty-four cents."

She glanced at what he held. Papa Juan's Fresh and Fast displayed across the box top. It was too early for pizza, unless someone was having it for breakfast. Sounded good to her animal. No, they were out here for their mate.

"Marika?" She turned to see a sexy man in a suit and tie step away from a dark vehicle in the next row. That was him. Better than what the phone showed. Again, her bright-green sneakers moved her forward.

God, he was so perfect. Maybe a bit too clean-cut and too neatly dressed, but that was fine. Mother Nature created each half for one another. Her research was all about this. None of that mattered now. She was meeting her mate.

He was meeting his mate. She was stunning. Her perkiness for him was so cute; he adored it. His eyes glanced over how her lab coat was buttoned wrong and how one pant leg was clinging to her sock, and her shoes reminded him of radioactive puke. He barely noticed any of that. She was perfect.

When she was near enough, he reached out and took her hand. Oh yes, the electricity and fireworks exploded in him. This was his mate, no questions asked. His arms involuntarily scooped her against him, bringing her flush with his body. She fit him, curve for curve. He breathed deeply and she did the same.

Her heart raced and his heart would forever match hers. One being. Of course, he wasn't saying any of that mushy stuff out loud. That was so not manly.

He wanted to kiss her, but that was going too far for the first ten seconds of knowing each other. Maybe not thirty, though. What should he say to her? *Hi, you're my mate. Let's get it on. Yes*, his panther said. He didn't even dignify that with an answer.

Maybe he should've asked Russel for tips. Wait a second. What the hell was he thinking?

"Hi, Devin. It's nice to meet you," she said. Her hands shook. Was she as nervous as him? You'd think he was in high school asking out his first date. He needed to play this cool and easy.

"Hi to you too." For fuck's sake, if that wasn't lame as shit. "I mean, it's really great meeting you. You're even more beautiful in real life than on that tiny phone screen."

Her cheeks reddened. How sweet. Was it too soon to fall in love?

"I'm glad you came down for a quick visit. My fox was hoping you'd be the one for us." She ducked her head and blushed further. "Is this too soon to say that?"

He brushed his fingers over her cheek. "I don't think so. Not in this case."

Her smile blew him away. "Good, that's good."

Charli's SUV pulled into the parking lot. Their nonexistent time was up. He sighed. "Looks like it's back to work for us."

"Do you get to take lunch?" she asked. He nodded. "Would you like to come to my mother's today for lunch? I promised her I'd visit."

Meeting the parents already? Holy fuck. He found that he wanted to. She must've seen fright on his face.

"You don't have to. It was—I thought—"

"No, I mean, yes. I'd love to eat with you and your mom. Call me later? I have to go." He handed her a card with his mobile number. She slipped it into her coat pocket.

"I will."

Behind them, car doors closed. "Hey, Marika and Devin," Charli hollered. "How's it going?"

"Great, Charli. Fantastic," he said. He leaned down and placed a kiss on Marika's cheek. She quickly reached up to hold his face, then laid a big one on him. No wimpy cheek kiss for his mate. No. She was fire, ready to burn. Let the scorching begin! Right after that, she watched him walk away, leaving her to count the time before she saw him again. She was turning into a wuss.

CHAPTER EIGHT

Inside the FAWS building, Marika led Charli and Barry down the hall toward the refrigerated rooms. She fanned her face, still hot from her quick meeting with her mate. Boy, was he hot. She couldn't wait to get him out of his clothes. Good god, listen to her. She sounded like a horny toad. Fox, toad, who cared?

Barry carried a huge black bag that contained the mysterious animal Charli had spoken about on the phone.

"Marika, slow down, woman," Barry huffed. "I'm carrying two hundred pounds of dead wolf here." Marika wanted to have it in cold storage while she went over her findings with the other two. They could look at the animal afterward.

"Sorry, guess I'm a little excited."

"A little?" Barry continued. "I doubt a herd of grasshoppers has as much energy as you do."

Marika spun around and walked backward just as quickly. "A *herd* of grasshoppers? Seriously?"

Barry frowned. "Like I have a clue what a bunch of those things are called."

"'Cloud,' love," Charli offered. "They're called a cloud of grasshoppers." They deposited the creature in the deep freeze, then walked through the lab door. She heard Charli snicker behind her.

"What are you laughing at now, Charli?" Since her friend had been with her mate, the woman was always happy. It wasn't that Mari was jealous—not anymore—she was just as happy too.

Charli said, "Oh nothing. I could just tell which side of the lab you've been working in."

Marika stopped. "What do you mean by that?" She looked around the room, then at her little area. Yeah, she'd agree there were more—a lot more—papers, books, chip bags, pizza boxes, and a soda can or five than anywhere else in the room. But dammit, she was working. Who had time to clean while trying to play Build a Bear Shifter?

She snagged a trash can on the way to her table. "Here." She thrust it at Barry to hold while she scooped handfuls of trash into it. "I can keep a clean house, if I want. I just usually don't want."

Charli gave her a big hug. "You know I don't care how organized you're not. Just as long as you're not helping me in surgery, we're great. Or in a hurry to find your car keys, or the TV remote."

Mari huffed. "Have you ever seen pictures of Einstein's desk? He said 'Organized people are just too lazy to go looking for what they want.' And 'If a cluttered desk is a sign of a cluttered mind, of what, then, is an empty desk a sign?'"

"That's good." Barry laughed. "Did Einstein really say those?"

Charli bumped him with her elbow. "Don't get her started. Einstein is her idol." Marika brushed her hand through the air as if to wave away all the nonsense.

"Let's get down to business, you two. We have some serious stuff to go over. Barry being the center of it." The scent of Charli's fear filled the air. Barry wrapped an arm around his mate and held her to him. Marika longed for the same from a partner. She then realized the silly banter just now was their way of coping with the scary news she was to tell them. That made her rethink how she would reveal the facts.

Changing her mind on her presentation, she hopped to the next table and dragged a comparison microscope front and center, then felt around and lifted papers looking for the glass plate samples.

"After you guys left last week, I scanned Barry's prints into the national fingerprint system and came up with nothing. Then I went through INTERPOL's databases with prints and DNA. Still nothing." She stopped. Well, shit. Where in the hell were those blood samples? They were there a minute ago. Good god, she'd lose her ass if it weren't attached.

"Where was I?"

"INTERPOL," Barry and Charli said together.

"Right," Marika said, talking and searching at the same time. "I also put his data through other databases few know about, and still nothing. So, I figured Barry was either not from this planet," she looked over her shoulder toward Barry, "just kidding there. Or had been living under a rock so remote, he didn't even have a Facebook account."

Final-fucking-ly, she found the glass microscope plates tucked safely inside a plastic container where they should be. See, she could be organized.

She placed a plate under each scope, focused the lenses, then stepped back. "Okay, guys. Take a look at these. One is my blood cells and one is human. What do you think?" She knew Charli would know the difference, but she needed this for what came next.

Charli nodded, then moved for Barry to look. "I've seen plenty of animal blood and human blood," the vet said. "But I've never seen shifter cells before. It's like half the cell is human and half is animal, fused together."

"Agreed," Mari said. "Which is really close to how shifters and humans intertwine physically. To go from one form to another, both cells need to be readily activated. Thus, cells being fused together makes shifting complete and whole." She switched out a plate. "Now, look at these."

Charli stepped forward and leaned down to the eyepieces. "Holy shit, Mari." Marika remained quiet, letting Charli fathom the meaning of what she saw. "The new sample is Barry's blood, I bet."

She clapped her hands together and did a happy dance. "You are correct."

Charli pulled away and paced, brows deeply drawn. Barry bent over the scope. "My blood sort of looks like a human's, except something is attached to each cell. Yours was half and half, Marika, and mine are two stuck together. And what are the shiny things floating around? What does that mean?"

Charli answered before she could. "It means you're not human. Anymore."

CHAPTER NINE

Marika leaned against the table in the lab at FAWS and watched the blood drain from the face of her friend's mate. She'd tried to make the blow easier to handle, but it didn't seem to have worked.

Barry looked at Charli, then at her. "What does that mean, I'm not human? What else could I be?"

Charli held onto his hand. "Barry, let me speak to your other half like I did in my office when we first met." Marika watched as Barry calmed. Then slowly, the two began to glow in their own soft light. The shimmer was faint, but there. The sign of true mates, Marika had no doubt. Charli released his hand, and they looked at each other with such love. Marika and her fox could only sigh, anxious to get their hands on their own glowing partner.

Her friend turned to her. "When I talk to Barry's bear, he's quiet and hard to reach, almost as if he's detached and I have to bring him in. Now I want to compare that to yours, Mari." Charli reached for her hands. "Hold onto mine." Marika grabbed on tightly, excited to see what the outcome was.

Immediately, her animal jumped to attention. *Ho, boy, Charliiiii. I love you so much and you're so much fun and I love being with you and—*

Charli's body stiffened with a jerk and then pulled away. Barry caught Charli before she fell backward. Marika frowned. "What's wrong, Charli?"

Her friend burst into a laugh. Between gasps of breath, Charli spit out, "And I thought you were hyped-up on mega caffeine. Your fox runs a million miles a minute."

She smiled. "Oh, I could've told you that. She can't sit still long, either. It's ADHD—Animal Deadlocked in Hyper Drive."

Over the lab's intercom system came a voice. "Ms. Paters, please call reception. Ms. Paters."

She looked at Charli. "That's strange. You're the only one who's ever visited me during the day." She bounced toward a phone to dial the front desk.

"Ms. Paters," the receptionist said, "there is a man here to see you. He says he's with the fellowship." That meant nothing to her.

"What's the fellowship?"

"I don't know, Ms. Paters." Marika picked up a hint of hesitation from the young woman.

"All right. Give me two minutes, then escort him to my office. Please let him know I have others with me."

"Yes, Ms. Paters."

Marika hung up and turned to her companions. "Someone is here to see me. He says he's with the fellowship."

"Oh, he works with me, then," Charli said. "We going back to your office?"

"Yes, we'll meet him there." Marika stored the glass plates in the safety container and left everything else as is. She'd be coming back to it shortly, anyway.

They hurried to her office. When entering, Charli shook her head.

"I know, woman," Mari said. "It looks like a paper atomic bomb exploded. But I know where everything is, so don't move anything."

Charli held her hands up in innocence and proceeded to the cleared sofa she and Barry sat on the last time they were there.

Marika heard the hall door open and figured that would be her guest, so she waited by her open office door to greet the man. For just the one person that the receptionist had referred to, there were quite a few smells, and feet walking. By her estimate, there were three others, and judging by the heaviness of the footfalls, they were men—big men.

The closer the group came, the more she smelled the young receptionist's fear. Why was she afraid of someone who worked with Charli? Unless that was a lie to lure them back to her office. Her training and safety protocols flashed in her mind.

Her company was very conscious of security and terrorist activity. They were, after all, the only lab in the world devoted to animal forensic sciences. And shifter research now. Several times a year, the company had lockdown rehearsals and role-played various attack-and-rescue situations.

With little thought to her own safety, Marika flattened against the wall next to the door and prepared for unwanted visitors. Her fox lent extra strength for speed and decisive blows.

"Ms. Paters?" the receptionist said, stepping over the threshold. As soon as the woman cleared the door, Marika grabbed for the arm of the male, flipping off the lights at the same time.

With help from her animal, she flung the guy against the wall. If she could capture him, then maybe the others would back down or at least cease to be a threat. A high-pitched scream rent the air, from the receptionist, no doubt. And then all kinds of shit hit the fan.

Able to see perfectly in the darkness, Marika leaped onto the man trying to get up after hitting the wall. They rolled into stacks of papers and books, knocking them everywhere.

Barry and Charli jumped up from the sofa in front of the desk, tripping into a chair, sending more file folders flying. True to a mate, Barry dragged

Charli to the far side of the room and kept her hidden behind him. His growls and her friend's shouting added to the cacophony.

The other three men stormed into the room, slamming into the screaming young lady who just stood there. They held a weapon of some kind. Marika couldn't make it out while fighting her intruder.

Shouts of "Turn on the lights," "Marika stop," "Don't shoot," and "Shut her the hell up," echoed off the walls. When the lights came on, everyone froze, and Marika quickly surveyed the situation.

Barry had Charli smashed into a corner, her friend yelling at him to move his furry ass out of the way. One of the intruders had his hand covering the receptionist's mouth, muffling her continuous shriek. Marika wasn't sure if the woman had taken a breath yet or not. And the two other men stood by the door, one with his hand on the light switch, both holding gun-like weapons.

Marika sat on the floor with the main man securely wrapped in a choke hold. He wasn't going anywhere. She and her captive were probably a sight. A five-foot-tall lady pinning a man at least six feet and a hundred pounds heavier to the floor. Her fox was really damn strong and faster than most shifters. She had this.

"I suggest," Marika said, "that you drop your weapons, or your companion's head will pop from his body like a whitehead zit." She noted the man's dark hair in front of her face. "Well, more like a blackhead zit." The men didn't move from their readied stance. Her prisoner moved his hand and the men backed down, placing their weapons on the floor.

Charli slid around the desk, coming to her knees in front of the captured man. "Colonel Rupen, I'm so sorry." Charli pulled at Mari's arms. "It's okay, Marika. I know him. You can let him go."

Mari narrowed her eyes and sniffed the air. No fear came from her friend nor the young lady who'd finally quit yelling. Barry stood behind Charli, so the bear could back her if drastic measures were needed once the guy was freed. Slowly, she released her hold. The man coughed and leaned away from her.

"Even though a bit late," her friend said, "Marika Paters, meet Lieutenant Colonel Rupen, the *head* of the fellowship program I work for."

Marika looked at the frowning man. "Oh shit." She jumped to her feet from the floor where she'd tackled and pinned down Charli's boss's boss—the big kahuna of the entire fellowship. "Colonel Rupen, I'm so sorry." Both Charli and she helped him to his feet. "I smelled our receptionist's fear and thought you had bad intentions for coming here with a group of armed men."

Looking him over, she understood the receptionist's fear. The guy was freakin' huge, and if he had worn a scowl when arriving with the three Secret Service–like men behind him, she'd be ready to piss her pants too.

"Please, call me Rupen. And I apologize, Ms. Paters, for our hasty and barging entrance. I just received some information and scurried to put a team together to get here as soon as I could."

Charli brushed off the back of her boss's shirt. "What happened to have you rushing here?"

He looked at Barry. "Him."

CHAPTER TEN

After Devin left his mate in the safe hands of his coworker, he headed for the senator's house. Time to get the investigation going. But the taste of his mate's kiss lingered on his lips. How could he think about anything else?

The image of the monster wolf lying on the autopsy table popped up. That answered that question. His panther had a bad feeling about the whole case, as did he. So many questions needed answers—answers he had to find before the other wolf killed again. Yes, *again*, he was sure of it, as was his cat.

The large house at 1711 Magnolia Avenue had a line of cars parked along the street. Seemed every person in the neighborhood was at the home. Great. This wasn't what he wanted, an audience eavesdropping for gossip.

Detective Gibbons mentioned earlier that she'd take care of informing Mrs. Hayseed of her husband's tragic animal attack and death. He wondered who got to the senator's wife first, Gibbons or the neighbor ladies. He placed his bets on the rumor mill.

After parking his SUV as close as he could, which was a block away, he proceeded to the fancy front door he'd driven past a few times since moving to Shedford. Before he even knocked, he was ushered inside and offered coffee, tea, or milk, plus a Danish roll or sweet cake to go with his beverage selection. He felt as if he was in the midst of a Tupperware party, with all the ladies buzzing room to room.

He asked twice to talk with Mrs. Hayseed, and both times a lady went to fetch her and never returned. This was getting out of hand. But the stories his supersonic ears took in were almost worth the wait. Some said aliens were the culprits, along with vampires, and some mystical creature he'd never heard of.

Guess the real story of an animal attack wasn't exciting enough for these ladies. Probably would be if they knew the truth behind the animal. They'd all have coronaries if the truth leaked. Then again, he wasn't sure he knew the real story yet.

Deciding he should search for the mistress of the house on his own, he wandered from one highly decorated room to another. The backyard was spectacular with a pool lined with rocks and waterfalls, expensive-looking furniture, two gazebos, a grilling kitchen, and a four-car garage. Wow, he needed to research how much senators earned annually. He should get into politics, if only he could stand the constant bureaucratic bullshit.

Coming upon ornate dark-stained double doors, he paused to peek inside. When opening one of the doors, he found the woman he was searching for quietly sitting behind a heavy cherrywood desk. He cleared his throat and slipped inside.

"Excuse me, Mrs. Hayseed. I'm Agent Devin Sonder working with Shedford City Police. I'd like to ask you a few questions, if you have a moment."

She looked up at him with dry, but red-rimmed eyes. "Yes, Agent, please have a seat. Can I get you a beverage?" She set down the picture frame she held and raised the half-full glass of water in front of her.

He raised a hand. "No, thank you. The ladies have taken care of that already." She gave a nod and sighed.

"Please ask your questions, Agent. I'll be as helpful as I can be, but please know that Earl and I don't—didn't talk much. He had his life and I have mine."

That was a sad marriage arrangement. What's the point of being married if the couple lived separate lives? Marriage was forever, but were they doing each other the disservice of keeping the other from finding someone who made them happy? Would he be contented if his and his mate's relationship was to produce kits and that was it? No. He wanted more.

"Mrs. Hayseed, have the Shedford police spoken to you about the attack on your husband this morning?"

"They have. But I was aware of the news before they told me. One of the ladies' daughters is a morning runner and saw the aftermath."

"Mrs. Hayseed, I'm going to ask some questions that seem to have no relevance to your husband's death, but I'd still like you to answer them if you can."

"Absolutely," she said.

"Does your husband have any enemies or someone who would want to cause him harm?"

She raised a brow and tried to stifle a wry smile. "Agent Sonder, my husband was a US senator. Of course he had enemies. Mainly the entire Democratic Party. Now, as to those who'd do him harm . . ." She paused. "I don't know anyone."

Not letting his thoughtlessness ruffle him, he went on with another question. "Was the senator working on any particular bill or piece of legislation?"

Mrs. Hayseed shook her head. "I don't know, Agent. I apologize. I try to stay out of that part of things. Believe it or not, I don't like politics that much." Perhaps it was just the money she liked, then. He couldn't imagine mating for material wealth that could disappear with the flick of a dropped candle on a carpet.

Devin closed his pocket notebook and sat back in the chair. The library they were in was very impressive, of course. He wouldn't expect anything less after seeing the rest of the house. Dark, leather-bound books lined shelf after shelf. He wondered how many the senator had actually read.

"You know, Agent Sonder"—he turned to see her pouring the rest of her glass of water into a potted ivy that looked a lot like the one he had found on his desk that morning—"there was a time when Earl and I spent hours going through many of these reference books, looking for legal precedents and results of trials that would give his clients a leg up.

"Those days are long past, but I still love my husband. Agent Sonder, please use any means necessary to find and kill whoever took Earl from me."

He swallowed hard. "I will do my best to uphold justice, Mrs. Hayseed." She gave him a sad-eyed grin. The woman understood what he meant and accepted it as how it would be. He would not step outside the boundary lines of the law to catch her husband's killer. Did she know it was a shifter who tore out her hubby's throat? For being a secret, the shifter world seemed to be known by a shitload of nonshifters.

She stood, and Devin followed suit. "Please look around his office here for anything that might help you." She gestured to a table covered with binders and what looked like rolled-up building plans or land surveys. "He did all his work in this room when home. Feel free to search cabinets and drawers as well. If he was hiding something, it's moot now."

Devin handed the older lady his business card. "Please call me if you think of anything that might help us in the investigation."

She smiled and slipped the card into her slacks pocket. "I will, Agent Sonder. Now, if you'll excuse me, I have a house full of gossipmongers to appease."

"Yes, ma'am. And thank you for your permission and trust to go through your husband's political dealings." She nodded and left the room, quietly closing the doors behind her.

He let out a breath and ran a hand through his hair. He had no doubt the senator was murdered. Whether by the wolf shifter that got away or a conspiratorial group, he didn't know. But Hayseed was guilty of something. He had to find it; he felt time ticking away.

CHAPTER ELEVEN

Marika stood beside her office desk while Colonel Rupen, the big kahuna, stared down Barry. Charli stepped in front of the bear as if to protect him.

"What do you mean 'him'?" Charli asked. "He hasn't done anything illegal on purpose. And—wait a minute." She looked at those in the room. "What does Barry have to do with you? You're not even from here."

This was so not good. Rupen's puzzled expression showed he had no idea what the hell was going on. Shit, where to even begin with the story.

"Who is Barry?" he asked.

"Wait." Marika jumped in before things got nasty again. "Hold up, there, big guy. You need to hear the entire story before you do whatever you came here to do."

Rupen's brows drew down. "What story? What are you talking about? We're here to take Perry Frid into custody."

Barry's body stiffened. Charli whirled to face him and asked, "Does that name ring a bell? Is that you?" Then she whirled back around to Rupen. "You can't arrest him. He's my mate." One of the three guards dropped his weapon that he had picked up, mouth gaping, eyes bulging. Rupen snapped his fingers at him, and the guy picked up his firearm.

The military commander narrowed his eyes and studied Charli and her mate. "If he is your mate, then you're saying he's a shifter. Perry Frid is one hundred percent human."

"That's probably true, sir," Marika replied. "But Barry, there, is one hundred percent shifter. Oh wait, I mean he's half-human, half-bear."

The head honcho wiped a hand down his face. "Okay, Marika, you better get started on that story. Obviously, there's a lot I don't know."

For the next half hour, Marika and Charli rehashed all that had happened in the past week, starting where Charli first saw the bear at a neighbor's farm, to the lab results they looked at thirty minutes ago. Barry's complete amnesia hadn't changed a bit. He was still as clueless now to his identity and past as he was then. Marika knew more about him than anyone else, since she had his fingerprints, blood, and DNA.

Rupen sat back in his chair and crossed one ankle over a knee, then gave a deep sigh. "So, Barry," Rupen said, "do you have any memories prior to meeting Charli?"

"Funny you ask," the shifter said. "This morning I felt"—he paused, looking for the right words—"I felt a tickle in my brain when sitting in the meeting at Charli's office. Like something wanted to burst forward, but couldn't quite do it. That's the best way I can describe it." He tightened his arm around Charli and hugged her closer. Marika sighed. How romantic.

The big kahuna squirmed in his chair, then leaned forward, putting his elbows on his knees. "Charli, Barry, we have a situation here I've never dealt with, nor have I ever come close to imagining such a scenario, it's so 'out there.'"

Marika watched Charli look at Rupen, then glance over her shoulder to her mate. "What could be that difficult to deal with? Barry's a great guy—"

"Stop there," the lieutenant colonel said. "That's the big issue. The Barry you know is not the Perry I know."

How could that be? Marika wondered. In school, she had studied the story about Sybil, an abused child who had multiple personalities.

Well, until it was exposed as a fake story made up by three women. Was Barry a different personality of Perry? What would happen if those two mindsets collided?

"Wait a minute," Marika nosed in. She turned to Rupen. "Who are you to know this Perry in the past? How long has he been gone? What is Barry to you? You going to kill him?" Her fox stretched, ready to take this man down again if he threatened her friend's mate.

"It's not like that, Mari," Charli said. Her eyes darted to Rupen. "At least, I hope it's not. Why don't you tell them more about yourself? It could help us all understand what you know about aliens and shifters better."

Barry gasped. Mari glanced back and forth between them like there was a ping pong match going on.

"No fucking way. Aliens?" Barry said. Mari bit her lip. Man, this secret-keeping stuff was hard.

Rupen shifted in his chair, looking like he was getting settled in for a long story. Mari so wanted to hear this. She was already studying the connection so anything he said would probably help her in her research.

"I am one of the commanders of a military unit that doesn't have a name. We do a lot of special ops that must be done under the radar, so to speak."

"Like the Navy SEALs?" Marika asked.

"Yes," Rupen said. "We often let the SEALs take credit for our work to help keep our identity quiet."

Marika's brow raised. "And what is your purpose here?"

"I'm glad you asked, Ms. Paters."

"Please, call me Marika since we're learning everyone's history."

"Thank you, Marika. I am honored," Rupen said.

Her brow went even higher. He was a smooth talker. And she had to admit, he was cute. But he wasn't "the one." She'd found her man. And now she needed to focus on Rupen or she'd slide into daydreams of her sexy mate.

Rupen looked at Barry. "We are here to take Perry with us to be debriefed on his past AWOL years. He's considered a deserter since he's alive. The military doesn't take kindly to a soldier who does that."

Charli huffed and crossed her arms, leaning against Barry's chest. He kissed her temple. Mari's fox sighed, thinking of her kiss with Devin. His lips were soft and demanding. Damn, she wanted to spend time with him. Lunch couldn't come quick enough. She shook her head to get back in the game.

"Here's what I'm struggling with." Rupen gave a nod toward her friend on the sofa. Marika caught Charli's worried eyes. Whatever this decision was, she felt Charli's whole world was about to change.

The man set his eyes on the bear shifter. "Perry—"

"Barry. I am Barry now. My past is what it is. I won't let it define who I am today and who I love. Whatever happened back then is over. Perry is dead."

Rupen sat back with his arms crossed. "Barry," he started again, "I have the ability to give you your past back. Question is how you will handle knowing the truth."

"Give it back how?" Charli asked, suspicion and fear rolling from her. She didn't seem to trust him even though he was part of her fellowship. But he was from the government, so . . .

Rupen cleared his throat. "Each of the men have a 'shutdown' trigger in case of capture. When they realize they are in the hands of the enemy, a part of their brain goes blank."

"What do you mean 'goes blank'?" Barry asked. He seemed more intrigued than frightened.

"Under hypnosis," Rupen said, "you were given a command to forget your past so the enemy could not access those memories to use against us. No matter the torture, you would have nothing to reveal."

"That's horrible," Charli cried. "You can't do that to people."

Stoic, Rupen replied, "We have for years and will continue to until another way to ensure the safety of our country is found. Now," he turned to Barry, "is it strategically better for me to unlock your brain here with Marika and Charli available for questions, or wait until we're back at HQ?"

Marika chewed on her lower lip, still analyzing the situation. If Barry did get his memory back, the biggest question was which personality would rule? Was he a good person or bad person? Being in the military, he may have killed lots of people. Could personalities combine into one? Damn, this was fascinating. What she wouldn't do to be in Barry's head, right now.

Seemed no verbal communication was needed between the shifter and his mate. Did they talk to each other's minds? The air grew thick with worry and concern. She'd need to open the door if this kept up. Those two emotions stunk the worst next to fear. Fear scented like someone crawled up your ass and died. Worry and concern smelled like farts. And in a cramped room, smelling like someone ripped a big, juicy one, life wasn't good.

Barry took Charli's face in his hands and kissed her, deep and long. After coming up for air, he laid his forehead against hers. "You know I love you, don't you?" Charli nodded, tears streaming from her eyes. "Nothing will change that. Together, we can deal with who I was and put that man to bed where he won't bother us anymore." Charli wiped at the wet drops on her face and nodded.

"Remember," he continued, "no matter what your eyes and ears may tell you about me, listen to your heart."

Oh my god, Marika thought as a tear escaped her eye. That line should be in a movie where the hero was about to risk his life to save the heroine.

Barry looked at Rupen. "What do I have to do?"

Rupen stood. "I will give you another trigger word that will 'release' your memories. But I warn you, Frid. You may not like the person you've been, especially since your disappearance. But it's as important for me to know where you have been as it is for you." Barry met him halfway between the furniture. "Are you ready?" Rupen asked.

"Ready as I'll ever be," the shifter breathed out. "Will this take long? I'm about to upchuck my breakfast onto your shoes." The big cheese of the fellowship quickly put his hands onto Barry's head. The room fell completely quiet, except for the heartbeats her fox's super ears picked up from the others. Or was that just hers pounding so hard?

Rupen leaned against Barry's ear. Marika heard a whisper of breath, but not what was said. Barry mumbled something she couldn't understand. His volume increased as his neck twisted. "No, no." Barry's body jerked, arms slightly swinging at his sides. "Please," he begged. "No." Barry fell to his knees. His voice carried from his bear, deep and scratchy. *"Take it back."*

Rupen stepped back and stood before the reborn man. Kneeling on a lump of papers, Barry dropped his head into his hands. Heart-wrenching cries came from Barry. Or was it Perry now? Either way, his hands balled into fists, his entire body trembling. His mumbling returned. He said something about his legs.

When Marika stepped closer, she heard the shifter whisper into his clenched fingers, "I am so sorry, Charli. Please find it in your heart to forgive me one day." With shifter quickness, Barry was on his feet and out the door. The guards aimed weapons at him in the hallway.

CHAPTER TWELVE

Devin stood in the middle of the deceased Senator Hayseed's home office, wondering how he should proceed. Usually in this kind of situation, he had only seconds to scour everything and get out before the bad guy returned. Now having all the time in the world, he hesitated. He hadn't realized how years of undercover work had molded him into the person he was.

He was completely different from the young, gung-ho rookie who couldn't wait to get to the station to start working. So much had happened over the years to kill that persona. Especially the past year and losing everyone he loved.

Pushing those thoughts away, he headed to the table that held files, books, and other crap. Sifting through file folders, he skimmed numerous legislative memos, letters, and propaganda from lobbyists. Seemed the senator focused on the oil and gas industry.

He flipped open a very large binder and read the front page: Deepwater Horizon Crisis. The four-hundred-page binder about the catastrophic oil spill in the Gulf of Mexico barely looked touched. He pulled on a cream sheet of paper sticking out of the back cover. The word Confidential was stamped across the top. In a plain font style with no pretty graphics or fancy color he saw DHC Classified. It read of a terrible event that plainly presented and proved the truth of the accident.

"Fucking figures," Devin said. He had every confidence the senator was involved in other events where the real story was also confidential. A rolled-up bundle of papers caught his eye. He cleared a space on the table and took the rubber band from the roll. His hands smoothed sideways, laying out the land survey. Placing binders on both sides, he was able to stand back and get an overview of the map.

The image displayed the upper western section of the country, from Seattle, Washington, to Sacramento, California. A red line snaked between the two cities. Glancing at the reference section to the side of the map, the red line represented a pipeline. Now the title of the map made sense: Sea-Sac Pipeline.

He flipped the sheet to the side to see what the next rendering was. The town of Shedford dominated the image, with the red line running mostly east of town through the hills and forests. But a small section looked like it might cross town limits in one location on the far southern outskirts.

Other pages showed various views of other towns and where the pipeline would be in relation to them. That was interesting, but nothing about it seemed illegal, especially since the project was still in the drawing stages. The last sheet, though, showed something else.

The names of the towns on the maps were listed on the left side with dollar amounts on the right. A yellow highlight had been drawn over Shedford and its money line. The dollar total was almost a half-billion dollars. None of the other towns were near that amount. The word Compensation was across the top of the sheet.

What in the hell was a town like Shedford going to do with that much money? Maybe something wasn't quite on the up and up with this project. He needed to find out who headed the project, who won the most from it, and who opposed it. After rolling up the papers, he replaced the rubber band around the middle and set the tube on the table.

From his sports jacket pocket, he pulled his phone. Clicking the icon for the Internet, he waited for the default search engine to load. In the search box, he typed in *Sea-Sac Pipeline*. There weren't many articles on the topic. A *Newsweek* report stated that such an idea was circulating, but the journalist doubted such a project would be accomplished with so much resistance from those worried about the environmental effects.

An oil-and-gas-industry magazine had an article describing the benefits of having a quick, easy means of pumping oil from the north, through the mountains, to California. According to the article, millions of dollars would be saved in shipping costs, and less greenhouse gasses would be produced. The project was spearheaded by an oil company in northern California.

He slid his phone into his pocket and made his way to the laptop on the desk. If he was lucky, the old senator would be one of those who left their computers on all the time, and didn't have a password-protected screen saver. He sat and wiggled his finger on the touchpad. The image on the screen disappeared to reveal Hayseed's personal e-mail. Hell, yeah. He loved people who weren't savvy in technology. It made it so much easier to snoop.

He clicked in the mail search box and typed in *pipeline*. Nothing. Of course not. That would be too easy. He tried *oil, Sacramento, pipe,* and a couple of other wild guesses and again, came up with nothing. Another tactic was needed.

Scooting the mouse to the left side of the screen, he clicked on Sent. A line of e-mails popped up. The last message was sent this morning, obviously before the senator went for his morning run. He clicked on it to open.

Continue with the project. I will send my account numbers for the deposit later today.

Once the transaction is completed, I will take care of the problem here.

Short and to the mysterious point. Could the project be the pipeline? Money was involved, probably a lot, if the town and money list was correct. What was the problem here? Looked like the problem took care of him first. He leaned back in the cushy leather desk chair and spied the ivy plant exactly like the one he had mysteriously received this morning and a landline answering machine.

He pushed the Rewind button. It was a message from a family member. He rewound another message, then listened.

"It's Klamin. Meet me and Shyler at the café, two o'clock."

Again, short and to the mysterious point. Who were Klamin and Shyler? Devin was willing to bet one of these people was the killer. Shyler . . . that name sounded familiar. Shit, did he know who the killer was?

CHAPTER THIRTEEN

Klamin sat behind his desk and pondered how to get his animal weapon out of the hands of the police before they got a chance to study it. Dammit. If they understood any of the implications, his plan would be blown to shit. And he refused to let years of research and work get pissed away.

He picked up his phone and speed-dialed the mayor of Shedford. When his soon-to-be high-and-mighty congressman answered, he started in.

"Shyler, I need you to go to wherever the weapon is being kept and destroy it before the humans get to it. You have access to all the city departments, right?"

"Hello to you too, Klamin." The mayor's sarcasm wasn't lost on him. "I went to the ME's office as soon as I heard the police brought in an animal. It's too late."

"Too late for what?" His anger built quickly. If he had to go up there, it wouldn't be pretty.

"The agent veterinarian from the fellowship had already taken the body. The ME gave permission when the agent explained a vet needed to do the autopsy."

Klamin's fist smashed onto the top of his desk. "Where did she take it?"

"Either her clinic or possibly the FAWS facility. I know shifters work in the lab."

"What the fuck is FAWS?"

"It's the Fish and Wildlife Service in Ashville. They are quite good at what they do."

He snorted. "What do they do? Fish all day?"

"Actually," the mayor said, "they have state-of-the-art forensic technology, and we've sent evidence to them several times to run tests."

Dammit. This was not what he wanted to hear. If they were any good, they'd be able to break down and identify the enhancements to the animal. Humans hadn't even yet discovered how to create the covering the fur attached to. And they never would without the alien material needed to create it.

"You don't have any pull there, do you?" Klamin asked.

"It's federal, so no. I can request shit, but they are under no obligation to comply."

He sighed. "Do you have a contact there? Someone with authority."

"Not really," the mayor replied. "But all the paperwork I see is signed by someone named Paters. This person probably holds some important position. Maybe lead scientist or head of a department."

He thought about what they could do to get to this person. A plan formulated in his head. "Shyler, call this person and nicely insist they meet with a fellow scientist setting up a new lab here in town. Their expert opinion and thoughts about the lab would be great. People love to give their opinion, even if not asked for. Tell them someone will call shortly with a time and location."

"Got it. I'll call you back with the full name and contact number for the person."

"Good." He hung up and sat back in his chair. He had to destroy the animal if he couldn't get his hands on it.

Others had no idea how many generations of mutated human-animal failures previous research teams, as well as he, had gone through. And then on the first test run, he fucking lost one of his best. How damn hard was it to kill an old man jogging in the woods? Granted, said man had a gun, but that was what the animals were created for. He needed to talk with his scientist to fix this weakness.

Dammit, Perry would normally be on his way to the lab to get Sloan for him. Now he had to go himself. Rolling his chair back and heading for the lab, he thought about having the idiot he had sent on the kill mission this morning call the scientist. No, he had to get Perry back. Even if he had to take out the female vet.

At least with Hayseed out of the way, he could put the mayor under his thumb. Shyler knew exactly what could happen if he decided to turn traitor. Shyler's first legislative move would be to stop that damn pipeline from going through his land.

His entire compound was hidden underground, and if digging machines, construction crews, and ground survey groups followed the current plans, they would work directly above his underground facility for several hundred feet. He couldn't chance them drilling or digging down and hitting his concrete bunker. But that had been solved, so he could get the crew back on schedule.

CHAPTER FOURTEEN

S top, don't kill him," Colonel Rupen shouted to his men pointing weapons at Barry's back as he ran down the hallway at FAWS. "Follow him." The lieutenant colonel stood at the entrance to Marika's office. If her eyes weren't deceiving her, she would swear he had aged twenty years in the last thirty seconds.

Charli darted out of the room, screaming for her mate to come back.

Marika sat behind her desk, stunned from such strong emotions thrown around. She had never felt how raw and ragged a soul could be. But watching a soul shatter tore her apart inside.

Deflecting her painful train of thought, she looked at Rupen frowning, sadness filling his eyes. She asked, "Aren't you worried you'll never find him again?"

"I want him alive. He knows who he is and will contact his base as soon as his head settles. He's programmed for that. I've informed his CO we might have found him and to be ready to move quickly to bring him home. They will debrief him and get back to me."

"Can't you just track him down and bring him back?" Mari asked.

He smiled the first genuine smile she'd seen on him today. "Sorry, he's a shifter. It doesn't work that way." Marika almost laughed at his words. How many times had she repeated that last phrase to the man in bed with her? Not that she slept with a lot of guys. She could count all her past lovers on one hand with two fingers left over. And for many months now, maybe over a year, she hadn't had sex with a man. Note that toys were not men. She'd had a few big Os with the assistance of Devine, her customized Sybian machine.

Whoa, hold the phone. Was it a coincidence that she named her toy Devine and her mate was Devin? It was so meant to be. He would become her Sybian machine very, very soon.

Thinking about sex snapped her out of the semidaze she was under. She heard Charli in the hallway crying. *Oh crap.* She jumped up from her chair and dashed into the hall. Her best friend needed her now more than ever before.

Outside her office, she flung her arms around her best friend and held her tightly. "You know he'll come back, Charli. He loves you." Charli nodded against her shoulder. "He's probably on system overload right now. His entire life came rushing at him, and apparently, it wasn't all good."

Her friend pulled away and wiped her eyes. "You're right, Mari. As always, using your brain and not letting emotions sweep you away." She wrapped an arm around her shoulders and squeezed for a second.

"Well, I don't know about all that," she said. "I'm just here to look at an ugly dead wolf."

Charli sighed. "We should examine the thing. If for no other reason than to keep my mind busy on something other than Barry. Plus, I could be called anytime for a pregnant cow."

"Pregnant cow, huh?" Marika said. "I'm doing scientific breakthroughs that will change our future, and you're leaving me for a preggers cow."

Charli laughed. "You know I'd choose you over sticking my arm up a bovine's butt and playing with her insides."

Marika stopped at her office door. "You so do not do that, do you? Your entire arm?" Damn, she was totally squigged out, bouncing on her toes and shaking her arms as if to shake off cow-innard goo. "That's just too gross, girl. I knew there was a reason I chose to work with dead animals."

"Yeah, like that's any better, rotting carcasses."

"At least I don't have to worry about it farting when my shoulder is tucked against its backside." Charli laughed heartily. Marika had achieved her goal of cheering her bestie from a broken heart to laughing over cows cutting the cheese in her face. They stepped into the office where Rupen waited.

Charli gave him the evil eye. "I'm not happy with you right now."

He looked at the floor. "I know. I'm sorry for that. I had no idea about the situation. Nor would I have ever guessed it."

"How did you know he was here?" Charli asked.

"When Perry disappeared," he started, "part of our process was to put an alert in several databases to let us know if that person had been entered into the system. When Perry's fingerprints registered, I got that information. I'm assuming Ms. Paters entered the data since her name was attached to the submission. A second hit on one print came in shortly after that."

"Yeah, that first set would be me. Well, we got an answer to who he is. Sorta." After an awkward silence, Marika called out to Rupen, "We're pulling a furry ice cube from the freezer. You want to tag along and see what we got?"

Rupen's face scrunched. "A furry ice cube?"

"Come join us, Colonel," Charli said. "I got something I bet you ain't ever seen in that military of yours. If you can stay, that is."

"You have my interest piqued, young lady. Lead on."

CHAPTER FIFTEEN

Marika laid the two-hundred-pound body bag on the lab table and unzipped it. Good thing she was a shifter, or she wouldn't have been able to carry the animal. Even with Charli's help. Then again, they could have asked Rupen for help too. Marika didn't need a man to do anything for her, except love and sex her.

"Okay, Charli, let's look at something *I'll* never see again." Marika pulled the bag from around the deformed skull and neck. "God, it's ugly. I hope I don't ever see it again."

Charli laughed. "I know, right?" Marika picked up a scalpel from the tray of tools she'd prepared. "I want to look at what this growth on the face is. It's very hard." She sliced off thin layers of material, and with tweezers placed the pieces in a fixative solution to preserve them, then dipped them into stain, finally putting them on a glass plate to view under the microscope.

"Wow," Marika said. "Look how dense the material is." Charli slid over to look in the scope's eyepieces. Then Rupen after Charli.

"I've not seen anything like this on an animal before," Charli said. "Not even cancer cells bond like this."

Marika asked, "Do you think this is natural or man-made?"

"If it was made by humans, what is the purpose of it on a wolf's face?" Charli asked.

"Perhaps it's some kind of protection. Like body armor." Rupen said as he stepped back to let Marika look at the material once again.

"Body armor," Charli said. "Never thought about that before. Then why not put it all over the body?" She glanced at the busted-out hole in the back of the head. "And obviously, there's little protection from anything that enters the mouth. That's how this damage had to be formed, in a straight shot through an open mouth, out the back of the head. The senator pulled off a trick shot before going down."

"So how did the senator die if he killed the wolf who attacked him?" Marika asked.

"Because there were two animals. The second got to the senator after he shot the first wolf," Rupen said. "Never send in one assassin, in case something happens. It worked to the killer's advantage."

Marika looked up from the scope. "Are you saying this creature was made to kill?"

Rupen remained quiet, lost in his own thoughts. She could only imagine what was going through his brain. Lifting papers and candy wrappers, she searched for the blood specimen she'd had before the fiasco in her office. Why was she always losing stuff? She found it next to a banana peel.

"This is Barry's blood and a human's." She slid the glass plates into place. "Okay, guys. Tell me what you think."

Rupen motioned for Charli to look first. "We saw this earlier. Barry's"—she paused abruptly and turned her head ever so slightly—"I mean, Perry's have human cells with a weird-looking cell attached."

While Rupen had his turn at the scope, Marika picked up a blood smear from the wolf. "Now, let's see who Mr. Wolf is." After removing the human blood sample, she slid the plate under the magnifying lens. Staring at the strange configuration, she felt relieved. It was exactly as she expected, but with a surprising addition. Saying nothing, she stepped back for Rupen.

Rupen bent over the scope and frowned. "It looks like Perry's. Human blood with a cell piggyback. I'm guessing the tagalong cell is the shifter part. Wait, the red liquid has little shiny things floating in it." After a moment of study, Rupen backed away. "I see. We have a couple different things going on here. Perry and the wolf have human blood with attached cells. Are you saying a human has been turned into a shifter with these extra cells being attached?"

Marika nodded. "That's my assumption. My cells are half and half, a born shifter naturally blended. Theirs are two independent cells linked, forced together into a man-made shifter."

"Ah," Charli said, "that would explain the differences between talking to Barry's bear and your fox. The bear was barely there, and your fox about blew me away, she was so strong."

Rupen sighed and rubbed his hands over his face. "Shit. This means we have a person trying to create shifters. But what's the shiny stuff in both the wolf's and Perry's blood?"

Marika quickly processed all she'd learned from the murder, Barry's situation, and the blood results. "It might be a trait belonging to the multishifter family." She turned to Charli. "Could Barry be a multi?"

Charli shrugged. "Could be. He didn't even know he was a bear shifter until I told him."

"I need a sample of a multishifter." She stood back. "Know anybody who is?"

"Our coworker Russel so happens to be a multi," Charli replied.

"Great. Can you or Devin get me a blood sample from him?" Marika asked.

"I'll text Devin and Russel."

Just the sound of her mate's name threw her heart into overdrive. She had to get out of here and to her mother's to see him. This blood stuff was exciting and all but would be here when she got back.

Charli sighed and leaned against the counter. "What does this mean? What is the purpose of this whole mess?" Mari's heart did a one-eighty flip when she smelled the anguish and sadness from her bestie. She didn't want to think of the fact that this was the best day of her life, finding her mate, and the worst for Charli, losing hers.

The lieutenant colonel cleared his throat again. "My guess is someone has created a weapon that blends in with nature to make it virtually undetectable to humans. An invisible killing machine."

Oh god. Mari didn't want to think about the implications yet. She needed to mate, then she could think again. *Let's get the show on the road*, her fox advised. She pivoted on her toes and speed-walked toward the lab door. "I'm hungry. It's time for lunch. I'll text you later. Bye." They knew where the door was. She didn't have time to waste. Her mate was meeting her for sex—oops, she meant lunch.

CHAPTER SIXTEEN

On her way to the car, Marika's phone rang in her purse. She pulled it out and looked at the caller ID. It read *Mayor's Office of Shedford*. Surely, this had to be a wrong number. "Hello."

"Is this Marika Paters at the Fish and Wildlife Service?"

"Yes."

"Please hold one minute for the mayor."

Her eyes popped wide. Why was he calling her?

"Hello, Ms. Paters?"

"Yes, this is Marika Paters. Please call me Marika, Mayor."

"Thank you. You are so kind."

"What can I do for you, Mayor?" she asked.

"I have a favor to ask of you, young lady. I've heard about your outstanding work at the Fish and Wildlife Service."

"Thank you, sir. But—"

"No need to be modest. You're great at what you do. And I would greatly appreciate if you would share your knowledge with a new business coming into Shedford."

"A new business? What kind?"

"It's a lab."

That's interesting. "What kind of lab?" she asked.

"Um, scientific-like."

As opposed to a nonscientific lab? Not very helpful. "What do you need me to do for them?" she asked.

"The owner would love your opinion on placement of equipment and stuff like that."

"Okay. I'm not sure how much help I can be since I'm not an interior designer—"

"No, no, no. Nothing like that. He just—Would you please visit with him for a few minutes today?"

"Today?" Kinda last minute here.

"Yes, this afternoon. Say around five thirty. They are on the south side of town, so you could be there quickly from your job."

She could be, if she really wanted.

"Please, Marika. He's a good friend of mine, and I'd like to help him and bring more jobs to town. Our people need to feed their families."

When he put it like that, how could she say no. "Sure, Mayor. I'll go to his lab. Where is it?"

"Oh, uh, he'll call you with directions. Is this number good to reach you?"

"Yes."

"Great. Thank you so much, Marika. I appreciate this." The line cut off. She looked at her screen to make sure he was gone. If that wasn't the weirdest conversation she'd ever had. How did he even get her name? Better yet, how did he get her cell phone? He was the mayor, so he probably had contacts everywhere.

She texted Devin for directions on where to meet and hopped into her car, ready to see her sexy stud again.

Devin texted info back to his mate. He was glad they were going together. Doing lunch was so new for Devin. He hadn't done extracurricular activities often in LA. Maybe got a beer occasionally after work, but that was it. He hadn't wanted to see those people any more than he had to.

At first he was into socializing and hoping to find his mate. Coming out of college, he was still in his partying years. Hooking up with non-serious women sometimes, but when his stepsister and her son needed a place to stay, that mostly ended. Which was fine with his panther, who didn't like the other women, but understood his human's physical needs.

Come to think about it, he hadn't had sex in quite a while. He had no interest in women, it seemed. Not one female had turned his head since he moved here. How could that be? He was as horny as the next guy. Wasn't he? Well, not as bad as Russel.

That man was a nut case when it came to females. Detective Gibbons had a challenge on her hands if she mated. But he wasn't too sure she would mate with Russel. She came across rather tough on his coworker, not even giving him the time of day.

There was something about the woman that saddened him. He didn't know if he picked it up from her smell, the look in her eyes, or what. Or maybe loneliness recognized itself in others. He shook his head to clear it. He didn't want to go down that road again. It almost killed him last time.

Devin left the car and glanced at the cute cottage in the woods. It reminded him very much of the Red Riding Hood story. He glanced at Mari, and joy bubbled in his chest. Fuck, he felt like a wuss, but he was so damn happy to have finally found her.

Mari jumped out of the car without waiting and rushed to him. She smiled brightly and took his hand. "Come on, my mom's going to love meeting you."

He cleared his throat. "Does she know I'm coming?"

Mari shrugged. "She won't mind. She's used to me forgetting to tell her things. Besides"—she leaned into him and pressed her warm lips on his cheek—"she'll love knowing you're mine."

The way she said the words made his panther stretch and push to get closer to their mate. He was most definitely hers, but she was his. Nothing and nobody could stop that.

"There's just one thing," she mumbled as they got closer to the entrance. "She's a bit odd with stuff, so don't feel weird with her way of doing things, okay?"

He wondered what the hell that meant. This was his first time meeting any woman's parents, and the fact this was his mate made the upcoming moment more important.

Once they reached the front door, Mari huddled closer to him and knocked. There was a silence before the door opened and a woman who looked identical to Mari, only an older version with her hair pulled back into a bun, smiled and held the door wide open for them. "You made it, darling! Come on in."

Mari tugged him inside the house and turned to face her mother. "Mom, this is Devin. He's my mate!"

The woman smiled even wider and pulled Devin in for a hug. "I'm so happy to meet you, Devin. My name is Ava. Please, make yourself at home."

Devin immediately felt welcomed into the woman's home. "Thank you, Mrs. Paters."

"Oh, honey, no. Please, call me Ava. Everyone does," she said, and led them into the cleanest-looking living room he'd seen since his own.

"Thanks for having us over, Ava."

Ava turned to face them in her pristine sky-blue-and-white-decorated living room. He loved the colors, the accents, and more importantly, how very organized everything was. "You have a lovely home."

She preened and sighed. "Thank you so much. I try my best to keep things in their places. It's kind of hard when Mari's dad is all over the house." She glanced at her watch and met Mari's gaze. "I'm about to put our food on the table on the back porch if you'd like to bring Devin that way. I'll get everything else out there in a sec."

"Sure thing, Mom. Do you need help?"

"No!" Ava cleared her throat. "That's not necessary, love. Show him the rest of the house."

He was alone with Mari again, a moment later. "I told you she was a bit strange."

He frowned. What did she consider strange? "What do you mean?"

She snorted and pulled him down a hallway lined with photos in matching frames and spaced exactly the same throughout. Devin was impressed with how perfectly put together everything was.

"She is super OCD about organization." They finally went through a set of French doors that led to a massive backyard, and Devin wanted to make an offer on the cottage right then and there. That backyard was a thing of beauty.

"Wow," he mumbled, taking in the sight. There was an iron pergola with a curved top covered in wisteria vines. It was massive, at least fifteen feet long, and there were so many vines and so much color on it, Devin could see his panther spending the entire day under it.

On the ground at the center of the structure sat a gorgeous wooden table that could easily seat twelve. Benches lined both sides with seat cushions in shades of purple to match the vines draping from the pergola. A simple white tablecloth covered the table that was set with pale lilac and violet dishes. Three antique outdoor lanterns were used as centerpieces, and more hung from the pergola above. It was the backyard of people's dreams.

"Mom loves coming out here, so she keeps this place super nice," Mari said. "My favorite is that chair over there." She pointed at a massive tree not far from them. From it hung a hammock chair made of what looked like thin bamboo limbs that allowed airflow through the chair. It was in the shape of an egg with a giant cushion inside and could easily fit two people.

"That's a great little spot she has there."

"Yeah. I used to love to study there when I was in school."

"All right, children," Ava said from behind them, "I'll be just a second and we can eat."

In the time it took for Devin to do another slow glance around the perfect yard and turn to the table, there were giant platters of food there. Two had lasagna. There was a big salad bowl with colorful vegetables in it. A big tray of fresh baked bread, and iced tea and lemonade in two different pitchers.

"Come on, let's eat." Ava grinned and waved them to the table. "If I would have known you were coming, Devin, I'd have made more food."

He blinked at the giant lasagna pans. "Thank you, Ava, but I think there's enough food here for at least six people."

Mari sat next to him at the table and Ava sat across from them. Devin wanted to congratulate her on how nice and organized her house and yard were. He had yet to see a leaf out of place.

"I just wanted to thank you for allowing me to join you both today," Devin told Ava. "This is very nice."

Ava blushed and smiled at Mari. "He's such a sweetheart. I'm so glad you finally found your mate, darling."

"Me too, Mom. Dad will love him when he finally comes out of his workshop to meet him."

Ava nodded. "Yes, he will. Devin, are you open-minded?"

He frowned. He liked to think he was, but he wondered now that she asked. "I believe I am."

"Good."

Mari smiled and piled food on her plate. When she reached for the salad with the bread tongs, Ava grabbed the salad bowl and moved it out of her reach. "Really, Mari. We've discussed that each plate has its own serving spoon."

"Aw, come on, Mom. They're all going to end up in my tummy anyway."

"No 'come on,' missy. Give me your plate." Ava held a hand out and proceeded to serve Mari's food without dirtying the tongs on different foods. Devin could kiss Ava. He had almost pulled the tongs out of Mari's hand himself.

"Devin, you're probably wondering why I asked about being open-minded."

"I am."

"It's because of me," Mari replied. "She's very tidy, and I'm . . . not. Well, I am, sorta. So she feels whoever my mate is needs to be able to understand I have my own way of doing things."

He nodded. "I see."

"Mari is very much like her father. They're geniuses with very little time for putting things in their places. At least that's what most people think, until you see them in action. Then you realize they work under an organized chaos that could drive a person like me insane." Ava chuckled. "Thankfully, I am very patient and learned to allow them their space while they made sure to follow my rules when in mine."

Mari bit down on a piece of bread and winked at Devin. "Don't worry, I'm not that scary. I'm actually a lot of fun."

Oh, he'd bet she was. In fact, he couldn't wait to find out just how much fun she was once he got her naked.

The rest of the meal went by in a flash of fun, easy conversation and anecdotes on Mari's teen years and her love for multiple colors in her hair. By the end of their visit, Devin was glad Mari was so identical to her mother in looks or he'd believe she was adopted. Her and Ava's personalities were complete opposites, but the love he saw between mother and daughter was unmatched.

"That was really nice," he said, back in the car as they drove away.

Mari licked her lips and blinked at him in a way that made his panther stand to attention. "I can think of something a lot nicer."

Fuck. He thought he'd been the only one thinking of sex but it appeared he wasn't. "Oh?"

She glanced at his mouth and then back at his eyes. "Yeah. What do you say we go back to my place?"

He'd say *hell yeah!* He had to play it cool. Appearing too desperate might turn her off. "If that's what you want."

She frowned, then grinned. "Oh, you don't want to?"

"Fuck, yes!" Damn, there went not sounding too desperate. "I mean, yes, I do."

"Then let's get out of all these people clothes and get to know each other better." Her words were followed by the ringing of his cell phone.

CHAPTER SEVENTEEN

O f all times for a damn phone call. He'd just ignore it and be with his mate. She glanced at him then turned her eyes back to the road.

"Aren't you going to at least see who it is?" she asked. He was curious, so he pulled out his phone to see *unknown* was the culprit.

"Doesn't say," he said.

"Maybe you should take it. It could be important. I'm worried it might be police work I shouldn't be hearing, though."

Her words hit him in the heart, reconfirming this was the woman for him. Back in LA, he'd heard numerous stories from the guys about why they didn't have significant others. So many, it seemed, were divorced. A hazard of his job was the potential to drive those he loved crazy.

Keeping secrets was no way to have a relationship, but he had new secrets every day he wouldn't be able to share with anyone. Wives found that hard to live with. Women worry. That's what they do. And if the husband isn't telling her everything, the wife knows. God knows how, but they know when men hold back.

With Mari understanding the position he's in—not able to divulge investigation information—they were more likely to stay together. She wouldn't be upset if he couldn't tell her how his day was.

Then a thought occurred to him: she was in the same boat. She dealt with criminal evidence and investigations on a regular basis. That's what her company did. He didn't like the idea that she couldn't tell him everything about how her day was. She could be lying to cover up something she didn't want him to know.

His panther slapped him upside the brain. *Stop thinking like a human man, for god's sake. You're getting stupid. She's your mate. Double standard much?*

His animal was right. He was being stupid. His mate would never even look at another man, much less want an affair. He planned on giving her more sex and love than she could handle. The thought of fucking her made him instantly hard.

The phone rang in his hand again. He pushed the talk icon. "Hello."

"Devin. It's Charli and Rupen here."

Marika nearly shouted, "Hey, Charli and Rupen. Long time no see."

"Yeah, yeah." He could see Charli rolling her eyes at them. He really enjoyed this group of people he worked with. He planned to be in Oregon for a long time to come.

Charli said over the phone, "Rupen and I are sitting at a nearly deserted Italian restaurant. You and Marika need to be part of this conversation we're about to have. You two are obviously together. I don't mean *together* together, but—you know what I mean."

His mate laughed. "If you are referring to us having sex, we haven't yet," Mari said. He liked that qualification. "We're on our way."

Charli groaned. "TMI, Mari. That's my coworker you're talking about. Now I won't be able to look at him and not picture you two having sex. Ugh." Mari and he laughed.

"What do we need to talk about?" Devin asked. He was ready to get this conversation over.

Charli said, "Rupen, I'm sure you already know Devin. He's another of the fellowship agents. He's in charge of the murder investigation and some other cases that may involve Bar—Perry."

"Hello, Devin. Nice to sort of meet you," Rupen said on the line.

"Nice to meet my first big boss too. Welcome to the circus."

A laugh carried across the line. "That it is." Marika groaned. He looked at her, but didn't ask.

"I was telling Charli a moment ago," Rupen started, "I had something similar to this new creature creation a while back in the DC area. It could've become very serious if it hadn't been discovered."

"Do you think this could be that bad?" Charli asked.

"I think it could be worse. Much worse."

Charli spoke up to them in the car. "Are you two going to listen, or do we need to send you home to get it out of your systems first?"

Marika grunted. "Of course we're listening. We have ears, don't we?" Devin couldn't take his eyes from her beautiful ones. She couldn't help but sigh at his calming scent.

Rupen's voice reached Devin's ear. He must be talking about Charli's mate, Benny or Barry. Whatever. He couldn't think of it, right now.

Rupen continued. "Your Barry is Perry Frid. He belongs to a group of men who are called on to do dirty work the government doesn't want people to know about." Charli's gasp registered in Devin's head. His mate's best friend was mated to a military man. Good for her. *Marika is so beautiful.*

They came to a stoplight he would've blown through had he not been paying attention.

Rupen mumbled something, then his voice came back. "His position in the group consisted mainly of sniper work. He's killed many people."

"But he was ordered to, right?" Charli sounded almost in a panic. "He didn't shoot people randomly. He wouldn't do that."

Marika took Devin's hand in hers and squeezed. He returned her touch, knowing she was feeling heartache for her friend. Marika glanced at him, and he nodded his understanding. She was such a great person.

Marika said, "We all know he's not like that anymore. Remember, the old him is dead, Charli. He's Barry, the man who loves you." Charli didn't speak.

Rupen continued. "Five years ago, Perry disappeared from the Afghan battlefield. Gone from the planet, it seemed. When we returned to survey the wreckage, we found his jeep turned onto its side. It'd come across an IED and flipped. We didn't find him, but we did find . . ." The lieutenant colonel paused. Both Devin and Marika wondered why.

"Found what?" Mari asked since Charli didn't.

"We found two partial legs trapped under the truck, which had been severed from a body."

Devin slammed on the brakes and pulled into a parking lot. He wasn't prepared for something that gruesome. His mate didn't look like she was either. Now the questions settled in.

"What has that to do with Barry? He has both legs."

"Based on DNA testing"—the lieutenant colonel sounded tired—"the legs belonged to Perry Frid."

"But how could that be? I don't understand."

"I don't know, but the man I saw in the office was Perry Frid." He paused. "Finding his prints in one of our system searches came as a huge shock. And discovering he's a shifter, I was even more floored. Something is going on here and we need to find what it is. It sounds more and more like someone wants to take over your world."

"Take over the world? What is this, *Pinky and the Brain?*" Devin joked. He noted that Rupen had been in his mate's office. He might have to ask about that. But until then: "Iraq tried to take over Qatar and got the shit stomped out of them. I don't see the world letting anyone take it over. We'll fight."

Rupen sighed. "You wouldn't win."

"How do you know?" A grumble came from his chest. Marika placed a hand on him, calming him.

"Devin, from what I discovered in my lab, they have technology we can't begin to counter without destroying the nearby area. Plus, I'm checking on a few other things."

Devin pulled her hand closer to him and kissed the back. His fear wasn't for himself, but her. He had to protect her, keep her safe from all the world threw at them. He couldn't fail her like he had his family.

"Rupen," Marika said, "what do you think about the wolf from the murder scene? Devin is in charge of the investigation. Anything that can help him?"

He couldn't believe through all this, she was still thinking about him and his well-being. He definitely loved her. She was sent from heaven.

"My thought," Rupen said, "is someone is creating a new type of shifter impervious to conventional attack. I'd like to study it more. Marika, may I bring in some of my people to work with you? They can relay your discoveries to me so you don't have to search out where I am."

"That will be fine," Marika said. "We can research together." She turned to her mate. "If you could ask Russel for a sample of his blood, I'd like to see if multishifter blood is any different than regular." Devin gave her a nod.

"But in relation to the murder, Devin and Charli," Rupen added, "I don't have anything to add yet. Marika and I will find out all we can."

Finding out about his mate was closer to what Devin was thinking. Getting to know every curve and dip.

Rupen continued. "If I'm correct, you two are going to mate after eating." Marika's cheeks heated, but the smell from her said she wanted the same. But that was how shifters worked. Nature provided a perfect other half, and there was no reason to question it. Hundreds of years and millions of matings were proof enough. So really, there wasn't a reason to be embarrassed.

Devin looked at her shyness and grinned a naughty grin. He was ready to end her dry spell.

Charli's voice seemed to be moving away. "Colonel, thanks for letting me know about Perry. And congrats on finding each other, guys. I need to get home in case my cow goes into labor. I'll see you at the hospital later, Devin. Good-bye, Colonel."

Devin felt grief and anguish pour from his little mate. "I wish there was something I could do to help her."

"Marika, there's nothing you can say or do that will make her feel any better. She knows the truth and has to find a way to deal with it. Hopefully Barry will come to her before he goes back to his base, and they can work things out."

"But what if she never sees him again?" His love was almost in tears. Her heart ached for her friend. He leaned over and kissed her temple. "She'll be okay, baby. Charli is a strong woman. She'll figure it out."

Rupen sighed. "Congrats on finding each other. I hear it's a somewhat rare phenomenon to find your other half." A grin spread across Devin's face. "Go on home now and get to know each other better. Marika, I might not make it to the lab later. With all that's happened, I need to consult with others. If I can, it'll be later this afternoon. Give me a call when you're . . . uh . . . free."

Devin had a feeling that Rupen was making up a bit of an excuse so his mate wouldn't feel rushed. That was fine with him. If he had his way, she wouldn't see the lab for a week. But that wasn't practical. He had just started a murder investigation too. Besides, she had a killing machine in her lab she needed to dissect.

CHAPTER EIGHTEEN

Marika instructed Devin to her home since it was closest. Man, the entire drive had been spent trying to get her animal under control. All she wanted was to get her hands on the panther and mate him.

Mate! Mate! Mate!

Mine! Mine! Mine!

If the damn fox didn't stop soon, Mari might have to jump Devin right there in the middle of the street. He pulled up to her house and neither spoke. Both jumped out of the car and rushed to the house. She jammed the key into the lock, turning it faster than she did on a Friday night ready for the weekend.

The moment they were inside, her arms went around his neck and their lips finally met in a kiss so desperate she almost forgot to breathe. He slid his tongue into her mouth, taunting hers. Flicking it around over hers and dragging moans and groans from her antsy fox.

God! She had never wanted a man like this. So desperately. So urgently. Like her entire existence depended on getting him out of his pants.

There was no time for her to tell him how to get to her bedroom. They stumbled onto the sofa, where he sat and she straddled his hips, rubbing herself over him like a fox in heat. She pressed her pelvis over his hard cock. Her pussy went slick with her need.

He pulled back from their kiss. His eyes were bright with his animal. "I want to devour you."

Holy fuck, those were the right words to say.

"Devour?"

"Hmm." He licked her lips and brought a hand down to the waist of her pants, unsnapping them and sliding the zipper down. His gaze locked with hers. "Tell me something, beautiful."

She gasped. "What?"

"When I finger your pussy, will you be wet? Will you be slick and aching, wanting me to slide into you?"

Hell yes! She wiggled on his lap, wanting to get a closer feel of him. She reached for his shirt, tugging it above his head and struggling to get the offending material off his gorgeous body. She had never realized how much a man's physique could turn her on until now.

Devin was hard all over. He was big and strong. And damn, all she wanted to do was lick her way down his abs to his cock. His arm muscles were smooth and warm. His gaze made her insides melt like butter under the sun.

He didn't have such a hard time with clothes. The soft sound of something ripping made her glance down to see his claws tearing through her outfit. In less time than it took her to thank him, she was naked in front of him. He'd slashed through all pieces of clothing, leaving her completely naked for his view.

She wasn't about to let him have all the fun, though. She clawed at his pants, ripping the material and getting him naked so fast her fox pushed at her skin excitedly.

"I haven't been with a woman in a long time."

She blinked. Not exactly what she'd been expecting to hear, but she'd go with it. "Okay."

His gaze pierced her. He didn't smile—instead, his face appeared carved in stone. As if just talking to her was taking up all his control. "No, you don't understand. Years ago, I fought my animal. I thought dating lots of women, humans and shifters, would mean I might find my mate." He lifted a hand and trailed his fingers from her jaw down to her neck. "It didn't work. I gave up hope and abstained from being with anyone else." His gaze rose to her eyes. "But now I found you."

She licked her lips, her lids wanted to shut at the sound of his raspy voice. His fingertips continued down, until they were cupping her breasts. "Devin . . ."

"Now I get you. My mate. Mine." He said the words with a possessiveness she hadn't expected but understood. Her fox felt the same about him.

"Yes, Devin. You've got me now."

"And I'm going to love being inside you," he rumbled, his other hand sliding between her legs and pressing at her clit. "Fuck! You are so hot. So goddamn hot, and I want to fuck you. I need you."

"Christ, Devin. The stuff you're doing to me, to my body. It's going to make me never want to leave this house again."

"Wait. This has to go," he growled. He lifted his hands and yanked at the band holding her long hair in a ponytail. The mass of blond strands fell down her back in a heavy curtain.

"I didn't care what my mate would look like, but you are so beautiful," he breathed. "I'll love watching your face when you come."

He rubbed the length of his cock over her wet folds and her world narrowed to only his body. He dipped his head and took a nipple between his lips.

"Fuck," she groaned.

Lord have mercy, his tongue was doing the Macarena on her nipple. It was making her pussy wetter and slicker than before.

No man had ever made her feel wanted so deeply before. She'd also dated human and other shifter males in her past, but none ever made her and her animal feel this out of control. Previous lovers had tried and failed to make her lose control. Yet here was Devin, and with a few kisses and touches, she was ready to come from how badly she wanted him.

She realized she'd been missing out. There was serious foreplay she'd never taken part of in the past. He sucked her nipples and glided his fingers in and out of her sex, driving her insane from desire.

She ached to have him inside her, dousing the fire coursing through her veins. She wiggled in his grasp, rubbing her pussy over his hard cock. Moisture from her channel dripped onto his shaft and coated him with her wetness. There was a crazy amount of heat spreading in her pussy. A heat that called for him to take her. To mate her. To finally give her that litter of kits she wanted so badly.

The thought of kits pushed at her control. Her fox wanted him inside her now, coming in her channel. She raked her nails into his hair, gripping the strands.

"Devin," she cleared her throat. "This might scare you a little."

He released her breast from his lips and glanced at her face. "What's wrong?"

"I am going into heat. This very second," she gulped at the wave of need and the instant desperation she could barely control. Her fox snapped at her to get it on already. "My animal wants kits."

He growled, lifted a hand into her hair, and fisted the strands, pulling her face to his. He kissed her hard, branding his ownership over her mouth. "I want my babies inside you."

Thank fuck! She didn't know how she'd manage to survive the night without begging him to come inside her. Now she knew she wouldn't have to.

"Don't worry, baby. I'll fuck you right and come so deep in you, we'll have those kits in no time."

She moaned and gasped when she felt herself lifted only to be put back down on the sofa. He put her on her knees, her chest draped over the back sofa cushions and her knees digging into the seating cushions.

He spread her legs apart and shoved her forward, his teeth nibbling their way down her back.

She gasped and dug her nails into the cushions, pushing her ass out toward him. He spread her ass cheeks open and she moaned. Good god, what the hell was he doing?

Her pussy throbbed. Fuck! She'd never wanted to come as bad as she did that moment. She was so wet she could feel her heat trickling down her thighs.

He continued his journey south, his cool licks popping goose bumps over her skin. He licked down her crack all the way past her hole and to her pussy. She bit down hard on her lip, closing her eyes and letting her body focus on just feeling.

He widened her legs some more and pulled her hips so that her ass was even farther out and easier for him to touch. He moved away, leaving her aching and needing. Suddenly he was back, his body coming under her to take his place on the sofa. He sat down, his face level with her pussy, and curled his arms around her legs, moving them so that they were now to either side of his shoulders.

She was glad he held on to her legs, to help her stay in place, because she would have slid down until she was sitting on his lap. His soft lips brushed over her pussy in butterfly kisses at first. Then he did a long lick from entrance to clit and started to fuck her with his tongue.

She could barely stop herself from shuddering as he lapped at her pussy like a starved man. He kissed and sucked, licked and fucked her sex until she was shaking from how close she was to coming. He flicked his tongue on her clit over and over again, licking circles around it. Her body held tense. She gripped the sofa so hard she heard the sound of material tearing. A quick glance down and she saw her nails had shifted into claws. Fuck. Not much she could do about it now.

All she cared about was having him continue to devour her pussy like it was the best thing since sliced bread. He licked, he sucked, but even better, he growled, and the vibration sent shudders all up her body. She could hardly contain the soft screams riding the back of her throat.

"Devin! God, Devin!"

"You like this, don't you, baby," he rumbled into her pussy. "Like it when I fuck you with my tongue."

"*Yesss.*" She would never deny that in a million years.

"Good. I can't wait to fuck your pretty little hole with my cock."

He slipped a finger into her sex, hooking it and rubbing the upper walls of her channel. Holy fucking god! She saw stars at that moment. But when he combined that with a hard suck of her clit, she almost came off his shoulders with a loud scream.

She rocked on his face, pressing her pussy to his mouth and wanting to drag out the pleasure coursing through her body for as long as possible. He licked her repeatedly, groaning in delight at the wetness her body released.

She glanced down at his head between her legs. Men had tried and failed to give her oral before. She'd been told it was a power thing. She had never felt comfortable enough to let go to the point she could orgasm from it. She'd been tense, and it had made for some awkward moments. None of that bothered her now.

The back of her sofa was toast. She'd need a new one. She'd scratched the shit out of it, but couldn't find it in her to feel even a little bad. When she tried to lift up, he stopped her. A soft inhale and he groaned. "Fuck, Mari. You smell so good. So ready for me to take your pussy."

She gasped when he rubbed his face into her swelling folds. Heat. She was in heat and she needed more of him. "Please . . ."

"Tell me to fuck you."

"Devin," she gasped.

"You know you want to. You want to tell me to fuck your tight little pussy and even your ass," he said, his voice pure churned gravel. "You want me to fill you with my cum."

Yes. She wanted that. The image of him doing just that made her blood run hotter than before.

"Tell me to come in your pussy and your ass. To slide my tongue into your hole and then my fingers. To work you into a frenzy and show you how fucking amazing it will be for me to take you from back there," he said, circling a finger over her asshole.

"Lord, Devin!"

He growled, sending vibrations through her body. "I'm going to fuck you now, sweetheart."

"Are you?" She breathed hard.

He slid from under her, making her get back on her knees on the sofa, still gripping the back of it.

He kissed the back of her shoulder and licked his way up to her earlobe. "Oh yes. I'm going to ram my cock into you. I'm going to own this pussy," he said, curling a hand around her hip and fingering her sex. "It, like you, is mine. I don't fucking share."

She didn't know why she loved hearing that, but her fox did a crazy dance at that moment. She didn't share either. He was her mate. Only hers. "I'm all yours. You're all mine."

"That's right, baby," he whispered by her ear, kissing her shoulder. "We belong together." He groaned and licked her again. "And now you're going to be all mine."

The head of his rock-hard cock slipped into her entrance.

"Oh my . . ." He wasn't even fully in her and she was stretching for him.

"Do you want me, Mari? Deep inside, branding you as mine?" he grunted by her ear.

"Yes. I want you deep. Take me. Bite me. Scratch me. Fuck me," she moaned.

He drove deep into her in one short thrust. He slid his rock-hard dick in and pulled back, quickly driving back into her. Fire burned in her lungs. She couldn't suck air in as he continued to pound harder and harder into her. He gripped her hips with his hands, his fingers turning into claws and digging into her flesh, leaving long razor-sharp scars on her hips.

"Oh god!" she screamed, her pussy grasping at his driving cock. She slapped her hand at his hips, scratching and clawing, trying to get a good grip so she could pull him deeper into her body.

"Mari, baby. You're soaked and so fucking tight. So tight and hot."

She lifted her ass just a little more so he would have an easier time getting inside her. Her muscles loosened up. Her mind focused on the feel of him stretching her pussy walls taut. He curled a hand around her throat, holding her still as he fucked her mercilessly. His body glided over her back, skin-slapping noises filling the house along with their mixture of growls and moans. He turned her face to his. She breathed roughly through her mouth, but that was soon cut off when he gave her a hard kiss that stole every bit of air in her lungs again.

His chest pressed to her back and the kiss turned flaming. Having his tongue invading her mouth at the same time he drove deep with his cock shut down all brain activity.

He curled a hand around her hip again, flicking her clit with two digits. Fuck! Spasms took hold of her core. She choked into their kiss, her pussy squeezing harder and sucking at his cock.

He grazed his teeth over her ear, sucking her lobe into his mouth. "I'm not stopping," he grunted. "Not until my dick is filling your slick little hole with my cum," he breathed. "Not until you're screaming my name when you come." His speed increased to the point it felt as if he were fucking her with a hot steel rod. "There's no fucking way I'm stopping until your legs are shaking, you can't move, and your pussy's leaking my seed," he growled. "I'm making sure tonight, we make those kits we both want."

The world shattered into crazy colorful fragments. She screamed, unable to control the call of his name rushing out of her throat. Her pussy squeezed his driving cock, harder with each spasm from her ongoing orgasm.

He thrust even deeper and stopped. His cock pulsed inside her, growing thicker by the second. A rush of heat filled her from the inside as he came. He growled on her shoulder, his body vibrating and still coming. It took a while for him to stop his tiny thrusts into her, filling her with his seed.

CHAPTER NINETEEN

Devin lay with his mate in his arms. They'd moved to the bedroom after their wild time on the couch. He loved smelling himself on her. And he liked smelling himself in her house. They'd figure out which place to keep later. He truly never thought this day would come, even though his mama swore it would. He knew how lucky they were.

Now that the pure lust of having to mate had worn off, his brain once again had blood flowing through it, and with it, logic. He remembered what happened to his stepsister and her son and immediately regretted tying this beautiful woman to him. She would end up dying because of her relationship to him. Then he'd be alone forever. His heart ached at the thought.

Marika rolled in his arms. "What's wrong? Why are you suddenly so sad? You're not getting rid of me, if that's what you're thinking." She was miffed. He squashed her to him. How could he tell her she had to stay away from him? Hide their love?

"Marika . . ." He did not want to say what he had to. "I have to tell you a story about me so you'll understand."

"Understand what?"

"Why we can't be together."

She rolled away, sat up, and crossed her arms under her chest, raising her succulent breasts. He couldn't help but lick his lips. *What was I going to tell her?* He leaned forward to have himself another taste, then a pain shot through his skull. He fell back onto his pillow. *What the fuck?*

"You're not getting one more thing until you tell me what you think is going to keep us apart." His eyes traveled to his lovely mate, holding her fist up. Did she just pop him one? "Yes, I bopped you on the head, and I'll do it again until some sense breaks loose and surfaces. Now get on with it. I want your cock inside me again." She grinned. Oh, she was being a minx, and his panther loved it.

Damn, he loved this woman already. Why was he pushing her away? Right, his story. He turned his eyes to the ceiling so he wouldn't be distracted by her lushness.

"When I joined the Los Angeles PD, I was young and eager to save as many humans as I could. Being a shifter, I excelled at hunting down the bad guys and taking hits with little injury. After a couple years of walking a beat, I was asked to do undercover work. Looking so young, I fit in well with the drug crowd.

"Being immersed in that society really beats up on a person. Fortunately, drugs and alcohol don't affect us, so I had no problems doing what I had to, to fit in. I facilitated many busts, with gangs going crazy trying to find the mole.

"The things I saw, Marika, would've crushed your soul. Torture, killings, stabbings, people so strung out they were on the brink of death, willing to do anything to get just one more hit." He closed his eyes and ran a hand over his face. This was the hard part. The part he didn't want to think about. His mate snuggled into him, giving him the support he needed to get through this.

"About a year ago, my stepsister and her son needed a place to stay, so I let them have the second room in my apartment. We talked to my nephew about not saying anything about me being a cop since I was undercover."

His mate whispered into his ear, "I bet he was really proud of you. Even idolized you."

He remembered the huge smile on little Jimmy's face every time he had come home. The young one wanted to hear everything that happened that day. Wanted to know how many bad guys he put in jail.

"I loved the child as if he were my own. He was a great kid." His heart wrenched at the memory of the dual-coffin funeral.

"What happened?" Marika said. She ran her fingers over his forehead, sweeping away the sweat beads.

"We're not sure how it happened, but I suspect Jimmy may have let something slip." His throat tightened, mouth dry. "I came home and found the apartment door open. Inside, I found the bodies of my stepsister and nephew . . . spread throughout several rooms." His mate's breath hitched and she squeezed him in her arms, nearly breaking his arm bones. God, it felt so good to have someone here with him. He used to imagine how it would feel having his mate hold him, but no fantasy came close to the truth.

"Turns out one of the gangs discovered I was a cop and took revenge on my family. And they won. I let them win. You know shifters can't get drunk. Our metabolism is too fast." She nodded. "Well, I did. Seems our systems can only take so much before it does get inebriated. Took several bottles of tequila slammed in record time. And shit, hangovers really suck. Don't get drunk." How he managed a little lightness with his last word he didn't know, but the love in his arms smiled. Which is what he wanted. Her to be happy.

"After that, I went to a dark place. A place I never want to go again. It was my fault they were killed. I gratefully passed out before I could poison my body further. When I woke, I was naked on the shower floor. I had no idea how I got there. Still don't. The worst part was the next morning, the papers and news reported a massacre at a gang stronghold. The same gang that killed my family.

"I have no memory of leaving the house," he recalled.

"What did your cat say?"

Devin laughed. "The genius little bastard gave the perfect nonanswer."

His animal bristled at the name-calling. Devin defended himself by reminding him that he had called him a genius.

"The panther said, *Be glad they're dead. Whether you did it or not, justice has been served.* He was right. A few months later, I was asked to take this job in Oregon. But I know my sister and her son were killed because of me."

"You don't know that, my love. If you hadn't given them a place to stay, where would they have been? In a homeless shelter, on the street? Child protective services could've taken the boy away from her. You can't say you were the cause. You just don't know. You made the last year of their lives happy and comfortable."

What she said made sense, but he wasn't going to forgive himself that easily. "What I failed to realize was she and Jimmy weren't strong enough to defend themselves against anyone who would come after me. I wasn't there to protect them, and they died because of me. That's why you can't be with me. I can't be here twenty-four hours a day to watch for bad guys coming." A perfect idea popped into his head.

"We can sneak between each other's places, making sure no one knows we're mates."

Marika sat up from hugging his body and looked at him. "That is the most idiotic thing I've ever heard. We are not sneaking out of windows like teenagers at their parents' home on a Friday night."

"But, Mari—"

She laid fingers on his lips to shush him. "So, you're afraid I wouldn't be able to defend myself if one of the bad guys came after me?"

He placed a hand on her flawless complexion. "I'm so glad you understand." He sat up and kissed her.

His mate flipped the covers completely off them. He loved her nakedness and slid his hands down her sides. She wrapped a hand around his neck, pulling him closer. Her other hand glided down his rippled stomach, following the V down to the promised land. But instead of wrapping her hand around his cock, she grabbed his thigh, then proceeded to launch him through the air to crash against the wall on the other side of the room.

CHAPTER TWENTY

Marika watched her mate connect with the bedroom wall. The drywall dented a bit, but she'd pay for the damage and the rest of the mess she was about to make. Better here than at his house.

Devin shook his head and got to his hands and knees. He looked at her with drawn brows. Using shifter speed, she jumped off the bed, raced to him, and grabbed him around the waist. With little effort, she threw him to smash into a chest of drawers.

"Marika, what the fuck are you doing?"

Saying nothing, she stepped into a cartwheel-back-handspring-backflip combo, landing on a dresser. She'd show him who couldn't protect themselves. She was going to beat the shit out of him.

She flipped off the furniture, landing in a crouch. Devin's eyes grew wider. Noticing his muscles tightening in his thighs and upper arms, she knew he was going to leap at her. Sure enough, he sprang.

Timing his flight, she waited. When he reached her, she rocked back, using his momentum to lift him enough to sail over her and crash to the ground. The floor shook. His anger filled the air. Now he was pissed. Just where she wanted him.

Marika dived on top of him, hands reaching for his neck. His arms caught her and they rolled against the bedside table. Her arm snapped up and took hold of the lamp. She brought it down toward his head.

He threw his forearm up to block, destroying the vase-style light. And that was fine. It was ugly, anyway.

Suddenly, she flew backward, landing on her ass. In a flash, she was on her feet, as was her ticked-off mate. They circled each other. When she got close to the door, she slipped out, put her back to the wall, and tackled her mate when he came through.

They landed on the wimpy coffee table and flattened it. Both were up quickly. Marika went on the offensive. She knew her mate wouldn't attack. But she really needed him to. She'd push him. Her self-defense classes with Charli, and karate as a kid, would finally come in handy. The idea of staying in shape was the original plan. She was a big girl, but able to control and use her weight to her benefit.

With kicks and punches, she drove Devin against the kitchen bar, yet she didn't stop her assault. She needed something more to push him over the edge. "Come on, Devin. Are you telling me my mate is truly a pussy?" She grinned at her own play on words.

"Marika? What the hell are you doing? I don't understand. We're mates," he pleaded. Both panted for breath.

"Well, let me tell you, *mate*. I refuse to be with anyone who can't beat me in a fight." *Yes!* She had him now. If he didn't fight to win, he thought she'd dump him. But he probably thought he couldn't hurt his mate. This would tell her who he really was.

Determination set in his expression. His body went from defensive to offensive. He came at her, arms and fists flying. She countered each and landed her own. Her foot stepped on something, making her lose her balance. Devin delivered a solid punch to her jaw, sending her against the front door. Terror poured from him.

His face turned to shock and worry, and he reached down to help her. "Marika, I'm so—"

She swept his legs, sending him to the floor, flat on his back. "Sorry is for pussies, darling. You're not convincing me you're worthy. I should leave your pathetic ass here on the floor. You should've stayed in

LA"—she didn't know if she should push this far, but she had a point to make to the gorgeous idiot—"and let your dark place consume you."

His head whipped toward her. Anger shot from his eyes and his hands fisted. Oh shit. Now she did it. She'd never battled so hard in her life, taking and giving. Her shifter speed was at max, blocking the whirling arms and legs trying to take her down. This is what she needed, what she wanted to prove.

She backflipped twice, moving out of his arm's reach. Both heaved for air. Blood and adrenaline coursed through her veins, bringing power and accelerated sensory perceptions from her fox. Her mate had to feel the same. Those good endorphins pumping up everything. She glanced at his cock. It was limp, as she expected. But twitched with her attention. She licked her lips and met his angry glare.

Now was the time. He could smell her want, smell her wetness. "What *you* fail to realize, baby, is that not every woman is weak or unable to defend herself. If you were human, I would've killed you a long time ago. Being a shifter is the only thing that's kept you alive, and barely at that." She watched his glare turn hot and desirous.

"You're correct, love. Now it is my turn to make a point." His cock rose to attention quickly. "And you're going to swallow it."

CHAPTER TWENTY-ONE

K lamin strode along the hall of his underground bunker toward the laboratory. He had to keep his plan in motion, keep everything moving forward. The most important aspects were encompassed in one large room, in the hands of his one scientist.

Sloan worried him. He shouldn't have granted the man access to cable TV. When not in the lab, the scientist was glued to the images and stories on the TV. A while back, Perry told him about Sloan's fascination with the supernatural—vampires and zombies especially. That made sense since the guy created creatures that belonged in that group. But lately, he wasn't so sure.

The man was old for a human, and occasionally, a nugget short of a Happy Meal. But the guy had made incredible strides in advancing the creatures. He made more progress within forty years than others had the entire centuries before. Of course, with borrowed technology from the much more advanced aliens. Klamin would show the government what happened when they told him no. His hand fisted and punched the wall as he continued on his way to the lab. Bastards!

Perhaps it was time to bring in a trainee. Someone highly intelligent, who loved research, and was young. He'd hit the jackpot if he could find someone who already knew a lot about shifters. The research facility the mayor mentioned popped into his mind. If this Paters person was a tech and not solely administrative, then finding a replacement scientist wouldn't be as hard as he thought.

Reaching the lab, Klamin stormed in. He searched the crowded room for the black mop of hair his scientist sported. The eerie beeps of the medical machines monitoring the silent, prone shapes lying under white sheets creeped him out. He didn't know how anyone working in this room remained sane. Which explained Sloan's mental state, for the most part.

Klamin stepped farther into the space, stopping by the first row of breathing experiments. "Sloan, where the fuck are you?"

The being lying on the table next to his side twitched and bolted up, the sheet flying forward off the body. Klamin yelped and jumped back, knocking another bed holding a covered body into machines, setting off screeching alarms.

The body sitting up launched at Klamin, instigating his reflexes to defend himself. His arm snapped out, catching his would-be attacker around the throat. Sloan's feet flew into the air as his neck remained firmly seized in Klamin's hand.

Klamin realized who he held, and immediately relaxed his grip, letting the scientist succumb to gravity and land flat on his back. "Sloan, what the fuck are you doing? You scared the shit out of me."

The scientist rolled onto his side, heaving in breaths. "Sorry, Master. I was up all night with the ivy and trying to sleep a bit before the next group sprouted." Sloan leaned against a bed to help him stand. Forgetting the beds were on wheels, he stumbled with the unit as it rolled into another, ripping the IV from its buried position under flesh.

A red splotch bloomed on the pristine white material, then as Klamin watched, slowly disappeared as if wicked back into the body it came from. That was interesting. "Sloan, what is this creature who retrieves its own blood?"

The scientist climbed to his feet and lifted the cover over the patient's head. "Ah, this is the antivampire prototype."

Klamin lifted a brow. Perry was right about the scientist's obsession with vamps and zombies. Klamin said, "I wasn't aware there were vampires to be the anti of."

Sloan ran around switching off alarms and quieting the room. "We must be ready, Master. Haven't you read stories the humans write about vampires ripping open throats and sucking out the blood?"

"I don't have time to read for pleasure," he said. "Just because shifters exist and humans write about them doesn't mean the rest of the garbage is real. Shifters are real because they were genetically engineered like all the other . . . things in this room. Have we created a creature specifically to live on blood?"

"Well, not completely."

"Then let's stick to the normal weird shit, shall we?"

Sloan was quiet for a second. "So, I shouldn't worry about the zombie apocalypse?" Klamin wanted to beat his head against a wall. The Paters scientist at the Fish and Wildlife lab was looking more and more valuable. "Sloan, please tell me our plants are coming along well. If not—"

"They are, Master. Come see." The little man shuffled around tables, boxes, and equipment to get to a desk almost hidden in a corner. He wiggled a mouse to bring the computer screen alive. Splotched in crimson like mud thrown onto the monitor, the word "redrum" flashed on and off. Sloan groaned and repeatedly pounded the ESC key.

Klamin stood back and crossed his arms. "What does that mean and why is it there?"

Sloan turned the computer off. "I don't know what it means. It just showed up one day and my computer freezes every time. I have to restart it."

"The word looks familiar," Klamin said. He didn't want to wait for the machine to reboot. "Show me the plants. I'll look at the data later."

Sloan led him through a door into a moist, tropical atmosphere. The room was covered in lush green vines and plants with large leaves. Overhead pipes sprayed water in fine mists. In a cryogenic container to the side lay part-human, part-plant bodies—remains of the latest failed attempts.

Sloan lifted an ivy generating from one stem in a bowl of water. "After those initial few shifters survived, I haven't been able to repeat the success yet."

Klamin's hand gently brushed a leaf. "Those first ones are working well. I can communicate with them most of the time. Their brains sometimes feel too weak for me to get what they've recorded in their minds."

Sloan thought about that. "Maybe it has to do with how much water is in the soil. Or it could be that plants go through cycles we don't understand yet. The sun may affect something. Have you noticed a pattern?"

"I gave the plants to the fellowship this morning before they showed up for work, so I haven't had long enough to find a pattern. Plus, nobody has been at their desk much today yet. But the senator has had his plant a couple days." That was how he discovered Hayseed's traitorous actions with the pipeline.

Sloan looked at him sheepishly. "Master, what if they are captured by the humans?"

"As long as they are under my mind control and don't shift, then they will never be discovered." His scientist did have a good point, though. He lost Perry to the veterinarian. "Just to be safe, implant self-imploding program directions in case they are caught. And be sure to do that with the next batch of shifters." After capture, their neurosensors would release the serum and virtually melt their brain matter. Made for much easier disposal; his lost bear had been a pain in the ass to try to kill. The only saving grace was that his memory hadn't returned yet.

Klamin stroked the leaf, smiling. Oh yes, his plan for this sweet spying foliage was progressing perfectly. His mind moved on to his ultimate dream. He was close after so many years and so many failed attempts. "What about our 'special' project, Sloan? Our time is running out. You must find a way to increase the speed of cell regeneration. If you don't, you'll find your way to the place where the first experiments are . . . six feet under, in the middle of nowhere."

"I need help, Master. Someone who understands shifter blood components and the genetics of the mixed species."

Klamin smiled. "Really, an assistant would help?"

"Yes, Master. Very much."

"Well, then. I know who can help you. You'll love her. We'll meet her later today."

CHAPTER TWENTY-TWO

Devin was glad she gave him a pair of her dad's sweats she kept at her place. It would look weird to get back to work with ripped-up clothing. Russel would never let him live it down. Once dressed, he helped Marika find her clothes. It was nearly impossible with her other clothes and shoes and girly stuff all over the place. Then added to that was the smashed lamp and flattened coffee table.

He didn't want to let his mate leave, but both of them had important things to do. They served the public in one way or another. Plus, he wasn't nearly as concerned about her safety at the lab knowing she could fight her gorgeous tush off.

After driving back to her vehicle, he kissed her until she was breathless, then sent her on the way to her lab. He pulled out his phone and dialed up Russel. "Hey, man. What you up to?"

"I'm starving. Have you eaten yet?"

"Just finished." Yes, he just finished eating his mate a couple of times. Delicious. Shit. His cock twitched. Not the time for that, buddy. "How about I meet you at the café on the corner of Magnolia and Tempest. I'll get a coffee while you eat."

"Yeah, that'll work well. See you then."

Devin hung up and slid his phone into his pocket. He had to get his head back in the game. He wanted to run what he found at the senator's by Russel. Even though Russ was a bit weird at times, he was still a great detective. He might come off as goofy, but Devin thought that was a cover for something deeper. What that could be, he didn't know. But he and his cat trusted Russ with their lives.

After the lunch rush hour, the café wasn't overly busy, allowing him to park close to the front door. He picked a table toward the back where they would have more privacy. A waitress wandered over and asked if he wanted anything. He ordered a coffee, extra cream for the cat.

Russel came through the door, lifted his nose, and turned toward him. Devin kicked out the chair next to him for his coworker. Russel sat and snuffled deeply. "So, Dev. Been *busy* recently? And I don't mean sniffing out the bad guy. More like the bad girl."

Devin's panther jumped forward, ready to defend his mate. He heard the humor in his friend's voice and calmed his animal. "Actually, she's a very good girl. And my mate."

Russel stared at him, looking skeptical. "You just met your mate? Here? In Shedford? Where? Who is it?"

"She's a researcher at a lab south of town. She's a gorgeous fox."

"Of course she is." Russel snorted. "She's your mate. Mine is foxy too, but we won't go there."

"No. I mean she's a fox shifter."

Russel scrunched his face. "A fox and a panther? That's a weird combo."

Devin's panther busted out a claw for the multishifter, seeing as Russel hated everything about cats. Devin was sure there was a hilarious story behind it. He lifted his arm, popping up his claws one at a time. Russel squeaked and nearly fell out of his chair.

"Dammit, man. You know I hate that shit."

"Sorry," Devin started, "the cat got pissed you called him weird."

"Control your pussy, dude." Russel's entire body shook. "I hate wild pussy. That shit is rank."

Devin laughed as his cat bristled again. "Order your food before more than a claw comes out."

"Yeah, yeah." Russel flagged down the waitress and ordered enough food to feed the department.

"How can you eat so much? You're skinny as hell, where does it go?" Devin asked.

"That's the thing with multishifters. We're different than normal shifters. Our metabolism is even faster than yours. When we shift into different animals, it burns more calories as the cells regenerate.

"I don't know the science behind it all. There isn't much information out there. Just stories passed down through the generations that clue us in to what we can do. There aren't many of us. I'm the first in my family in a long time. I think my great-great-grandma was the one before me. I got some fox jokes. Wanna hear some?"

Before Devin could say no, Russel started in. "Why did the fox cross the road?"

Devin rolled his eyes and played along. "I don't know why. Tell me."

"To prove to the possum that it could be done!" Russel laughed. "When does a fox go 'moo'?" Devin just shook his head. "When it is learning a new language!"

Yeah, he'd had enough and was about to say—

"Wait. How about these: Girl, if you were a dinosaur, you'd be a Foxasaurus. If I was a fox, I'd jump in your hole!"

These were worse than his rat jokes. And his cat didn't take kindly to the "hole" pun. Thank god the server came out with a large tray holding several plates.

She set the load on a nearby table and brought two plates over. "Who ordered the lasagna?" Russel lifted a hand. She sat the plate in front of him. The Salisbury steak plate in her other hand came Devin's way.

"Oh, he ordered that too." The waitress looked at him with a blank stare, like she didn't understand what he had said. She quickly snapped out of it and set the plate next to Russel.

She grabbed a plate of mashed potatoes and a plate of green beans, then looked at Devin. He nodded to Russel. Without missing a beat this time, she put the plates around his fellow agent. Next came white and brown gravy, a basket of rolls, and an additional drink.

Devin stared at it all. "Man, your mate is going to freak out the first time you go on a date and eat. If I'd ordered anything, we'd have to get a bigger table."

"Hey, don't hate me because I'm beautiful and get to eat this much," Russel said.

Good thing Devin didn't have coffee in his mouth or it would've been all over the table. One thing he could expect from Russ was the unexpected. Fortunately, while cramming food into his mouth, he was quiet. The only time he was quiet.

Devin scooted closer. "I need your help with some spying."

Russel sat up higher in his chair. "Absolutely. What are we doing? I have my camo face paint in the truck along with my heavy-duty disguise suitcase."

He had to grin, couldn't hold it back. "What is a heavy-duty disguise suitcase? Or should I not ask?"

His friend rolled his eyes. "Don't tell me you never went undercover before."

A ping of sadness hit his heart, but he wasn't letting it show. "I have, but as myself."

"Wow, that must've been boring." Russel scooted the plate of mashed potatoes closer. "My kit has everything you need to disguise yourself in public. Eyeglasses, crooked teeth, fake noses, mustaches and beards, wigs, hats. Then there's the periscope, cipher wheel, spy glasses, invisible ink pens, and disappearing ink—"

"Okay"—Devin lifted his hands, stopping the nonstop list of weird items—"I get it. Sounds like a kit I'd buy my nephew for his tenth birthday."

"Yeah." Russel smiled. "I got it for my twenty-fifth. Mom always knows the perfect thing."

Devin sighed. "Sorry, man. This will be along the boring lines. We need to talk with the mayor." He proceeded to tell Russel about all the things he found in the senator's office a few hours ago, including the answering machine message naming the mayor and someone named Klamin.

Russel chewed and thought for a moment. "So you think the senator was into something with the mayor and the Klamin guy?"

"Yes," Devin said. "We need to find out what it is, and if it's strong-enough motivation for murder."

"Do you think this pipeline thing plays a role?" Russel asked.

Devin drummed a finger on the table, scowl on his face. "I'm not sure. It seemed like a big deal with the newest info on the table. Everything else was from the past. And money is always a powerful motivator. If Shedford were to get the amount listed, the town's coffers would be filled. Well, that is, if most of it doesn't go into someone's pocket. Which I think might be the case."

"I agree we need to talk to the mayor." Russ wiped his mouth with a napkin. "You ready to go?"

Devin's eyes snapped to the table and the stacked, empty plates. "Holy shit, man. Where does it go? Your stomach can't be that big."

"Eh, it's used to getting a lot at once. I'll pay the check up front. Let's go. I gotta keep busy so I don't think of my mate."

Devin frowned. Same thing for him. He couldn't protect his little woman from a distance. It would drive him crazy. "Oh, wait." Russel turned back to him. Devin grabbed a handful of napkins from the dispenser on the table.

"What?"

"Stick your arm out," Devin asked.

Russel complied without asking why. With catlike speed, Devin slipped out a claw and sliced the offered limb. Before Russel could react, he slapped the napkins over the wound, collecting the blood.

His coworker tried to snatch his arm back. "What the f—" Those sitting nearby looked at him. He moved closer to Devin, not looking happy. "What the hell, man?"

Devin pulled the napkins away and pulled more from the dispenser. "Marika wants a sample of your blood to compare to the others she has." He wrapped the clean napkins around the bloody ones and stuffed them into his pocket.

Russel huffed. "This is not the best way to get a sample. Besides, you could've warned me first."

Devin smiled. "Naw, then you would've complained."

"Moi?" His coworker stepped back and laid a hand on his chest. Devin would be impressed if Russel knew French. But he probably heard Miss Piggy say it and learned it there. "Complain? Never. And before you ask, it's the only French word I know. I watched the Muppets as a kid."

"I got your blood."

Russel snorted. "I think we should redo that sample at the hospital, where they're trained to get blood without being masochists."

CHAPTER
TWENTY-THREE

Marika sighed as she drove back to FAWS. She couldn't believe she'd found him, or he found her. Whatever. She was thrilled. She hadn't wanted to leave after their quickie hour of sex. But she'd get more, much more, tonight. Hopefully, she wouldn't have to beat the shit out of him again.

Men could be such dumbasses. Their macho *protect the little woman* syndrome got tedious quickly. But that was part of being a shifter. That was as deeply ingrained as the need to sexually join. To breathe.

Then her mind turned to her current mystery—the wolf.

Was the animal a continued project, bred for the strange traits shown on the body? What clues did the rest of the anatomy give? If this was a creation, who was creating it and why? She needed to text Rupen to let him know she was on her way to the lab. She wanted his insight on the creature.

In her purse, her phone rang. Maybe she wouldn't have to call Rupen after all. The cell's screen had *unknown* across the front. She normally wouldn't answer a call like this, but the mayor had said someone would call her. Maybe this was them.

"Is this Marika?"

"Yes, who is this?" she asked.

"I'm Nex Sezol. I believe you spoke to the mayor earlier about helping out a fellow colleague."

"Yes, Nex. Glad to meet you."

"Same here, Marika. So I called to give directions and work out a time to meet today. Since we are on the south side of town, we're closer to your facility, which makes it easier for us all. I know you're working all day"—and all night, she thought—"so perhaps something around five or five thirty would work. It will be very quick, I assure you." He rattled off an address she committed to memory.

"Again, thank you, Marika. I look forward to meeting you tonight."

After hanging up, she wasn't thrilled. This impromptu meeting kept her away from her mate that much longer. She had about three months of vacation time earned. It was time to take at least a week.

She should have Devin do the same. With the murder investigation, though, this might not be a good time. She would do everything she could on her part to figure out the mystery behind the ice-cubed wolf. If they had another killer shifter running around free, they needed to stop it before it killed again.

She thought about Devin and her heart did a little flip. It was still weird getting all these emotions for a person all of a sudden. The longer she spoke to him and got to know him, the more she realized he was a good man. He was smart, tough, and now that she'd kicked his ass, he respected the fact that she could take care of herself.

Still, all this instant love and concern for him was wreaking havoc on her ability to stay focused on the job. She worried about him. She wanted to spend time with him. To get him naked and ride him like an untamed bronco at a rodeo.

She was happy, though. She'd been alone for so long and wanted someone to share her life with. A mate. Someone that truly connected with her and understood her. A man that would give her the kits her fox wanted so badly and the love she deserved. A smile worked her lips.

She'd enjoy this. Him. It was new, yes, but she would adapt and learn to be the partner he needed. They'd make this work.

CHAPTER
TWENTY-FOUR

After calling the mayor's office and being told he was working from home, Russel and Devin circled the block his house sat on and saw a small doggie door on one of the side doors. That would be perfect.

"Okay, here's the plan," Devin said. "I'm going in to talk to the mayor about the murder. Just short and sweet. You sneak in and find a place to hide nearby. If he's in cahoots with anyone, he'll call them after I leave. That's where you listen in. I'll pick you up down the street."

Russel started stripping. "That'll work. I'll go in the doggie door as a skunk so I can zap the dog if it gets too close."

"Perfect." Devin rolled down the window for Russel to jump from. "And look both ways before you cross the street. The last time, you got sucked into a street cleaning machine and scared the shit out of me."

Skunk Russel waved a little paw like saying, *Don't worry 'bout it. I got this.* Devin could only hope so.

He watched the cute critter scamper across the asphalt to the other side, then lost him in the vegetation. Time for his part. He stepped out of the car and made his way to the front door of the large, fancy house. It wasn't as gaudy as the senator's, but close. He looked around for the skunk, then pushed the doorbell.

After a moment, a woman he didn't recognize opened the door. He pulled a business card from his pocket. "I'm Agent Sonder working in conjunction with the police." He handed the card to her. "I'd like to speak to the mayor for a minute please."

She invited him in to wait by the door while she disappeared down the hallway. He took that time to look around. The walls were painted a light gray with black-and-white accessories here and there. It was much more modern than the senator's, airier also. No sign of a dog yet.

The lady stepped into the hall, followed by the mayor. She continued up the stairs, and the mayor zeroed in on him. "Agent Sonder, how are things in your department? I haven't been able to get over there yet to congratulate you for solving the robberies last week. You did a great job, son."

Ugh, he hated when people called him "son" or "boy." In most cases, he was older than they were. Just didn't look it.

"What can I do for you, Agent?"

"I'd like to ask you a few questions about the senator's murder this morning."

He looked taken aback. His face paled a bit. The man was definitely hiding something. "You don't think I killed him, do you?" Then the big man laughed and slapped him on the back hard enough to sting.

"Of course not, sir. I would just like your thoughts on some things."

"Absolutely." Devin received another knock on the back. "Let's go into my office. Don't want to disturb the women today. They're doing some heavy-duty cleaning before closing up the house for the winter. Airing out the rooms upstairs and such."

They settled into comfortable chairs in a masculine environment. Strong, bold colors, with a hint of cigar smell. "So, Agent, what can I help you with?"

Devin took out his little pocket notebook like every good detective did. Even if it was a bullshit act, it looked professional.

"Sir, do you know of any enemies the senator would have?"

The man smiled. "You do realize he was in politics, right?" He spoke as if it were a rule to have enemies if in politics.

"Yes, sir. I mean anyone more than usual." He slowly drew in a deeper breath to sample the air. The mayor knew shifters existed, but hopefully didn't completely understand all they could do. So far nothing concerning floated around. He did get a hint of fresh outside air. The mayor had said the women were upstairs airing out the rooms.

The mayor shook his head. "Not anyone I can think of."

"What about anyone the senator particularly didn't like?"

The mayor flattened his lips into a thin line. "I don't understand the question, Agent. Why would that be pertinent?"

Yeah, that wasn't one of his better questions. He was too focused on listening for Russel. "Mayor, do you have a big or little dog?" he asked.

"My wife isn't a dog person. She has a cat."

Devin swallowed wrong and coughed. Shit. The mayor asked, "You okay, son?"

A crashing sound came from the other room. The man behind the desk frowned, but didn't get up.

Devin asked, "When was the last time you saw the senator, sir?"

Scratching sounds in the hallway, like sharp claws on a wooden floor, passed on the other side of the door. Then a screech from a cat.

"That damn cat again." The mayor sat back. "It's been a while since I've seen Earl. We're very busy men."

Too busy to go into the office, obviously. On a side file cabinet lay a roll of paper like the one in the senator's office. He had already asked one stupid question. Why not one more. "Mayor, have you heard anything about a pipeline coming through the area?" The acrid scent of fear stung his nose. That was interesting. Maybe there was something to this pipeline.

The mayor looked at him without expression. "I'm sorry, Agent. Wasn't the senator attacked by a wild animal? I'm not sure what these questions have to do with his death."

A scream from somewhere in the house shot both men to their feet. They ran into the hall and heard a second scream. They ran upstairs, down the hall, and into a room with bed sheets and a heavy-duty carpet-cleaning machine on the floor. Two women stood against the wall screaming and pointing to the other side of the room.

On the other side, the cat sat on the windowsill of the open window, reaching out, trying to swipe a skunk bobbing from the end of a narrow limb. Every time the branch brought it up, the cat jabbed.

Oh shit. Devin didn't know what to do. He hurried to the window, shooed the cat, closed the pane, and turned his back against the glass, hopefully hiding the skunk behind him. "Well, that's interesting." The cat swiped at his leg. That pissed off his bigger cat. He looked down at the fluff ball, let his panther's teeth come down, and hissed at it. In a streak of white, the little cat disappeared under the bed.

His eyes glanced at the women across the room. They were still hysterical, the mayor trying to calm them.

"Mayor, this looks to be a bad time. I think I've asked all my questions. I'll let myself out." He left the room, not looking at the window. Russel was on his own.

CHAPTER
TWENTY-FIVE

Russel jumped from Devin's SUV, scampered across the street after looking both ways, and headed into the shrubs encircling the yard of the fancy house. He didn't see a dog anywhere in the yard; it must be inside. He'd have to watch for it.

He scuttled to the little animal entrance and pushed on the door. It didn't budge. He pushed harder. Still nothing. Well, shit. He hoped this wasn't one of those doors that only opened when the transmitter collar was close. Even if that was the case, he should be able to muscle his way through.

Backing a few paces, he prepared to put some elbow grease into it. Well, more like skunk shoulder into it. Charging on all four feet, he hit the door, prepared to bounce back. Instead, the barrier gave way and he flew through, hit the floor on the other side, and slid into the wall, feet in the air.

Whoa. The room whirled. He shook his head to clear the cobwebs. Still lying on the floor, he opened his eyes to big angry gold eyes hovering over his. Long white teeth happened to be below those eyes. Very sharp long white teeth. Before he could roll over to get onto his feet, a hiss blew in his face, flattening the fur. Damn, someone give that pussy a mint.

He slapped his bushy tail in the cat's face and scrambled to his feet. Not knowing where he was going, he ran like a bat out of hell for the first open doorway. Sliding around the corner, he entered the kitchen. The remains of beef stew and cornbread lingered in the air. Smelled really good.

A sharp pain trailed up his tail. Behind him, the cat had a mouthful of black fur. Shit, he needed to move faster. Maybe he should get on a different level. Coming around the corner of the center island, he leaped for the countertop. Being so low to the ground, he couldn't see what was on the counter, which happened to be the sink with lunch dishes stacked inside.

Immediately recognizing the danger, he was able to avoid the potential disaster. But the cat jumping up behind him didn't. It slid into the sink, slamming bowls, silverware, and glasses up and over the side to crash to the floor. Russel squeaked a laugh and an extremely pissed-off puss with beef stew on the side of its face glared at him. Damn, if looks could kill—

The cat launched from the sink, claws stretched, reaching for him. He scrambled backward and fell over the side. He landed on his back, but if he hadn't fallen, he'd be a cat chew toy right now. Why did it always have to be a cat. He hated cats. Everything about them. He needed to focus.

He was supposed to find a place to hide to listen to the mayor's phone call after Devin left. Well, he wasn't so sure that would be feasible. In fact, he wasn't so sure he would even make it out of the house without flashing someone with his junk. He headed out another doorway, cat once again on his tail.

Spinning out on the slippery wooden floor, he scrabbled down the hallway. He smelled Devin behind a closed door, but couldn't really stop in and shoot the shit at the moment. Damn cat. Coming up on the stairs, he noticed they were covered in carpet. That was what he needed. He could get traction there.

Swinging around to the front of the steps, he set his claws into the looped material, but his back end kept sliding until it bounced against the wall. The cat followed his path, squishing his ass end for a second before he took off up the stairs.

At the end of the hall, he saw an open door and smelled fresh air. Giving all he had, he muscled toward the room where two female smells came from. He tried to make his entrance as stealthy as possible, which was *not at all* with a pussy caterwauling.

When they saw him, both women screamed. He expected that. Nobody wanted a skunk in their house. A stabbing pain flared in his ass and he fell sideways, rolling toward the bed. He smelled his own blood. Damn cat got him.

Regaining his feet, he jumped onto the bed and ran to the other side, cat still following. He controlled his fall to the floor and ran under the bed, then hopped onto the bed again. The cat was smart, or his own tail dangled over the edge, giving away his location. Either way, the cat was on him like white on rice. And he was getting tired. He was just a little guy with little legs.

If worse came to worst, he would spray the cat, but in order to do that, he had to stand still. As soon as he stopped running, the cat would bowl into him with claws and teeth. He needed to keep on the move. Then he saw it.

An open window became his ticket to freedom. Aiming for it, he pushed the animal further; putting the fear of God into someone could really get them moving. Along with a bit of survival instinct. Reaching the window, he launched off his back legs, touched down on the sill, then shoved off one last time, grasping for a tree limb.

His tiny paws wrapped around a narrow, flexible branch, which, to his dismay, bounced up and down with his weight. The cat sat on the windowsill and swiped at him every time the branch dropped or raised him within reach. This was not good.

If he dropped to the ground from the second story, he could break a bone. Being naked in human form with a broken bone in the backyard of the mayor's house would probably make the morning and evening news.

In the room, Devin and the mayor came running in. Devin saw him and he breathed in a sigh. Saved. He stuck his tongue out at the cat and watched as his partner closed and blocked the window. Now, how the hell was he getting out of this? He still bobbed from the limb twenty feet in the air.

An idea came to mind . . . if he could shift fast enough, he could change into a bird before he hit the ground. *If.* It was as bad a plan as anything else. What the hell. He mentally prepped for the shift, then let go of the branch. Air rushed past him as gravity took a death grip. He felt the change mold him into wings with a body attached. Instinctively, he maneuvered for a sharp right-turn ascent. Pulling that many Gs would make a pilot pass out and his brains ooze out his ears. But his bird brain was safe.

Climbing on a current of wind, he soared over the tree and the house. On the street out front, he saw Devin drive away. He needed to find the mayor's office window and perch. Diving toward the side of the house, he found a set of bay windows with the mayor on the other side. He landed on the brick shelf outside the sill and listened in.

After the man hung up, he launched into the air. Devin was going to shit when he heard what the bad mayor was up to. Flying over the house, he saw that damn cat sitting in the yard, staring up at the tree he had been in. He'd teach that feline who not to mess with.

Taking careful aim, he gauged the distance and time. Reaching that perfect point, he dropped a bowel bomb and hit the pussy squarely on the back.

He hated cats.

CHAPTER TWENTY-SIX

K lamin left the lab and headed back to his office. He needed to eat lunch. It was well after noon. Where the fuck was Nex when he needed him? The moron would never be worth what Perry was. But what did he expect? He purposely designed that generation of shifters not to think, but to follow orders. A good army didn't consist of independently thinking individuals. Nip that shit in the ass.

When he entered his office, his desk phone was ringing. He hurried in, hoping to get there before the caller hung up. He needed to create a damn phone that worked underground.

"Klamin here."

"The fucking fellowship knows about the pipeline," the mayor whispered.

Klamin sighed. "Chill the fuck out, Gerald. They can't possibly know—"

"Bullshit. Devin Sonder was just here asking me about it."

"Why was he there?"

"He said he had some questions about Earl's death. I knew this shit would blow up in my face. Goddammit, Klamin, I swear—"

"I said chill out, Gerald. You don't want me getting mad. The senator got off lucky with what could happen if I get pissed off with someone. He got greedy and stupid. Don't do the same. You will take over Hayseed's political position and ensure our agreement remains intact. And when the time comes, you will have more power than you ever imagined."

The man on the other end of the line calmed. "Sorry. I'm just upset about Sonder coming here. I'll make sure the pipeline runs along the other side of town. Don't worry. Nobody will find your bunker."

"I'd better not have to worry," Klamin warned.

The mayor sighed. "Did you get the water set up? I saw the fellowship caught your girl."

"No, goddammit." He slammed his fist onto his desk. "The fucking fellowship has got to go. It's been a pain in my ass this past week. They've more than fucked with my plans."

"You want me to do something?"

Klamin sat back in his chair. He thought of the pros and cons in bringing in another high-profile person. "No. I have something else in mind that will lead to the end of the fellowship. I may need help in a couple days to deal the last blow, but for now, leave it."

"What about Sonder?" the mayor asked.

"Don't worry about him. I'll take care of it."

"That reminds me, Klamin," the man said. "I'm not pleased that you took care of the armored truck robbery without letting me know about it. I don't like people being uselessly killed. That money belonged to the people of my—"

"Would you prefer the money come from your own pocket? I could contact your political donors—"

"No, Klamin. I just want to be aware of things going on in my town."

"Yes, Gerald. You'll be updated on my plans now that you're my man. Don't let me down, or you'll be seeing Earl again." He hung up, tired of talking to the human idiot.

Humans seemed to be the bane of his existence. Why the elders had to crash-land on this godforsaken planet a thousand years ago he didn't know. But at least he was able to find their hidden ship and transport the shifter experiments to this compound.

Now his finest creation was almost complete. His army would soon be walking. Then no one, human or alien, would be able to stop him.

The phone on Klamin's desk buzzed. Shit, now what? He sat in his chair. "Hello."

"Klamin, this is Yugo Harzoon. What is your status? I am tired of waiting."

Klamin grimaced. This was one of the fucking Russians he didn't want to speak with. Harzoon was an arrogant ass that he would love to do away with, but couldn't. Harzoon was his only way into the black-market trading route where everything from technology to slaves were bought and sold.

"Yes, Harzoon. I know you want the merchandise, but your patience will make you very wealthy." That's what Klamin wanted Harzoon to believe, anyway.

Harzoon huffed. "It better, Klamin. I'm risking my neck the longer I continue this facade of goodwill with your government." The plan was for Harzoon to visit the United States under the guise of improving relations after the presidential election.

"I know, Harzoon. I appreciate your willingness to sacrifice now for the immense pleasure your newly gained wealth and power will bring you after we are operating." *Fuck*, he hated groveling and sucking someone else's dick. His time would come.

"Don't blow smoke up my ass, Klamin. It's not you. Tell me where we stand. I heard rumors that the military has initiated a special force to deal with paranormals on Earth. How will this affect us?"

Goddamn it. How did he hear about that? *Fuck*. He didn't want to deal with this now. "That is just another group of incompetent shifters and humans. Don't worry about this group, Harzoon. I have them firmly under control. I actually have plans for a few of them." Personal plans to start his harem. The Charli female was quite desirable with her narrow waist, wide hips, and strong thighs.

"As long as you handle the situation effectively, I won't intrude. But the first breath I hear that rings truth, you're on your own, Klamin. Understood?"

"Yes, Harzoon. Understood."

"Also, let me remind you that many of my patrons in several well-armed countries have prepaid for your . . . merchandise. If they don't receive delivery, they will come looking for you."

CHAPTER
TWENTY-SEVEN

Devin closed the front door of the mayor's house behind him. He thought about sneaking around to the back where Skunk Russ dangled from a tree limb, but thought better of it. Russel was a big boy and could get himself down. Besides, he didn't want to squeeze the skunk too hard and get the smelly shit on him. That shit was seriously not funny.

He crossed the street to his SUV and made to drive away, but only went down a block, U-turned, and parked to wait for Russel to return. He rolled down his window to catch his scent better.

His mind immediately drifted to his mate. He couldn't believe he found her. His mother was right. Fate would lead him to her. He was afraid of what he had to lose by bringing her into his life. Love for his family had always been strong. Losing his parents, one at a time, had almost killed him. But his younger sister still needed someone to watch over her until she finished school. That kept him going.

Shortly before he was born, his human mom was diagnosed with ovarian cancer. She refused any type of treatment until he was delivered and then had a hysterectomy as his infant self was cleaned up. She went into remission for several years and then his adopted sister, Lacy, came into his life.

The girl was six years old to his twelve years. She had been classified as one of those problem children, prone to hissy fits, who was hard to love. But his mom and dad had more than enough love to drown her in it. That seemed to do the trick. She never acted out, never caused big problems . . . Well, he thought that now, but at first she had been a hellion.

Until she was convinced they weren't giving her back, she fought everything his parents did for her. That could only be expected. His sister was hurting and lost inside. Even at such a young age. He wanted to help her, but he didn't have a clue what he could possibly offer a little girl.

Several days after she joined their family, he came home to find her throwing things in her bedroom and destroying everything not attached to the floor. He was completely baffled by her actions and finally asked her what she wanted.

She burst into tears, not saying anything. She flung herself on her bed and cried into her pillow. He sat on the edge of the twin mattress and rubbed her back like his mom did for him when he was sick. Her tears slowly became hiccupping breaths.

He and his parents had discussed not showing her their shifter abilities until she'd been with them for several years. That way she'd be less likely to share that information with others. But something inside him, maybe the cat, said *tell her now*.

"Lacy," he said while she still lay facedown on her pillow, "I don't know how you feel, and perhaps you don't know how to express it except as frustration, but I want you to know I like being your brother. I like having you in the living room and playing video games. I like having you ride bikes with me. You've made my life better just by being here." She remained quiet.

"Because you're my sister, I want to tell you something I've never told anyone else." This got her attention and she sat up.

"You want to tell *me* a secret?" Her eyes teared up, but for another reason. "Nobody has ever told me a secret before. All the girls would whisper and laugh at me, then run away. No one wanted to play with me. And *never* share a secret with me."

He nodded. "Well, I have a *big* secret. Only mom and dad know. And I only trust someone who is part of my family with it." Sitting cross-legged on the bed, her head tilted down as she picked at the Dora comforter.

Then quietly she said, "I want to be your sister, but I don't know how." From that moment on, life changed in the Sonder household. Laughing and joyous yells filled the house as the threesome became four, united by a shifter family's secret that bonded hearts. The secret of being a shifter.

All was well until his father was killed in the line of duty. Their town was small and, being tucked away in a rural area, had little crime. But they weren't immune.

A group of thugs decided they wanted to cut loose and cause a little havoc around the area. Devin's father, the town sheriff, wasn't too keen on that idea. He'd seen what had been happening to neighboring towns and was ready the night the crew came to visit.

What his father didn't know was that the group had added a couple of more shifters since the last time they were out marauding. Two bear shifters. When they entered town, they spread out to cause as much havoc as possible. His dad didn't want anyone to get hurt, including the dickheads making problems. But things escalated and shots were fired. Shifters shifted. Both bears ganged up on his dad and brutally took him down.

But his father wasn't a pussy by any means. His massive panther damaged the other two enough so they eventually died from their wounds. He simply couldn't stop his own bleeding in time to recover.

The FBI got involved after that since the group crossed state lines, and they were all prosecuted.

His mom moved them out of town, closer to her family in California. With the loss of her mate, her health declined quickly and the cancer returned. She passed shortly after his high school graduation. Her last words were for him to be patient. His life would pass by quickly. Fate would lead him and his sister to where they needed to be, to their mates.

With help from family, he and Lacy remained together while he went through college and the police academy, graduating with top honors. He was an adult even though barely twenty-three years old.

His cat brought his attention back to the real world with a warning that something was about to happen. Devin looked in all his mirrors for trouble, but saw nothing. He smelled nothing out of the ordinary—then a squawk exploded in his left ear as a bird dive-bombed through his driver's side window the same time that a fluffy-ass cat sprang from the bushes.

CHAPTER
TWENTY-EIGHT

W hat the fuck?" Devin's arms flailed as feathers and air whipped past his face. If his seat belt hadn't strapped him down, he'd be out of the SUV.

The bird's feet landed on the passenger window, then it sprang into the backseat. Bones and tendons popped and crunched as Russel morphed to his human form.

"Mayer, goddammit. Warn me next time. I'm expecting a skunk on the sidewalk, not a bird in my face. My cat likes birds, you know."

"Man, do *not* talk about fucking cats."

Devin burst into laughter and turned the ignition key. "Yeah, when the mayor said they had a cat and not a dog, I knew it wouldn't be pretty."

Russel sighed. "Fuck pretty. Fuck me." Devin glanced in the rearview mirror at his exhausted partner.

"A bird was a good idea. Should have thought of that first off."

"No shit, man. I'm retiring as the first to go into buildings. Let someone else deal with the damn cats. I'm doing clean-up from now on."

Devin laughed again. "Did you get anything after I left?"

"Did I? Holy shit, dude. We have a conspiracy right here in little Podunk, USA."

"Conspiracy?" Devin asked. "On what?"

"A lot of things. I'm not even sure what half the stuff I heard meant," Russel replied. "Are we going to the office?"

"We need to meet Charli at the hospital to see the cat woman."

"Oh yeah, forgot about her." Russel put on his clothes. Good thing. Devin didn't care to see his junk any more than he had to. Which should be never.

"Start at the beginning of the conversation," Devin said. "Did you get the name of the person he called?"

"Yeah, some guy named Klamin."

Devin slapped his hand on the steering wheel. "I knew that bastard lied. He stunk up the whole room with his pansy-ass lies. Klamin is the name on the senator's answering machine. Has to be the same one. How many damn Klamins do you know?"

"None. So sounds good to me." Russel stretched out in the SUV's middle seat. "The mayor mentioned your name. That can't be good, man. You might have a target on your back now."

Devin cursed to himself. He had to convince his mate to leave town until this Klamin guy was captured. He wasn't taking any chances. "What else?"

"I heard Hayseed's name. Now that he's gone, the mayor could take his place as long as he follows the agreement. What that agreement was, they didn't say. But they said something about the pipeline. And something about the mayor having more power than he could imagine."

"More power?" Devin asked. "What does that mean? In politics?"

"From what I've seen, there is no power in politics. Only the secret organizations with lots of money have power, unless you're talking about a dictatorship."

That was an interesting thought.

Russel went on. "Then the conversation went in another direction and I think this solves some questions for us. The mayor asked if Klamin got his water set up. The response wasn't good, going by the man's expression on the phone."

"You think he means the water utility? Was cat woman trying to bury an account for him so he didn't have to pay for water? That seems like a strange thing for someone to want," Devin said.

"Says to me that he's doing something with water he doesn't want anyone finding out about." Devin had to agree with that. There was always a reason, and usually it was money.

"The mayor also got on Klamin for the armored truck robbery. Apparently, Klamin didn't inform the mayor of the planned attack," Russel said. "That says to me that Klamin was responsible for the scheme and has the money in his possession."

"Yeah, it does look like this Klamin is in the center of it all. We need to find out who this person is." They slowed for the turn into the hospital's parking lot. "Mayer, don't say anything about Barry to Charli."

"Why not?"

Devin sighed. "That's a whole clusterfuck, but Barry is a professional killer—"

"Excuse me? An assassin?" Russel sounded incredulous.

"Um, yeah," Devin managed. "It's complicated, but Rupen said Barry is from his group."

"Well, I'll be a horse on shit. Why not mention it to Charli?" Russel asked.

"Obviously, Barry wasn't an innocent person in his previous life and when he learned of his past, he ran from Charli. I don't know if they've talked or not. So best not bring it up right now."

"Yeah, I can see why." Russel's concern filled the truck's air. "Seems you're the only one having luck with your mate. I really need to get mine to come over before my place gets dirty again. I haven't even used the downstairs bathroom. Keeping it pristine. No mold or anything that moves of its own will."

"Dammit, Mayer. You can be disgusting." Devin laughed. "You'd better not tell her that. She'd never allow your children in the bathroom alone." He parked the SUV and they headed for the main entrance. Russel was quiet the entire time. Devin opened the front glass door, letting his partner in first. "What's up? Why so tight-lipped suddenly?"

"It's nothing. Just been doing some thinking about my life and the future with my mate," Russel said.

"That doesn't sound good. You're not giving up on her, are you?"

"No, it's not that as much as making her happy."

"What does that mean?" Devin asked. "I'd do anything to keep Marika happy."

"Yeah," Russel said. "It's just that I realized I don't think I want kids."

Devin stopped in his tracks. "Why not?"

Russel shrugged. "It's a long story, man. One you don't want to hear. I'm worried that it will keep my mate from wanting me. Maybe she already knows and that's why she's playing hard to get."

Devin laughed. "She's not playing, dude. She *is* hard to get. And who knows, maybe she doesn't want kids either."

"Come on," Russel said. "What woman doesn't want kids?"

Devin turned to him. "My advice—unless you're really, really against something, let her have her way. If she wants kids, suck it up and get it up. Otherwise, shut up."

His coworker smiled. "I like that, man. Kinda rhyme time and all." His smile faded as he sank back into thought. Devin could only hope fate was on Russ's side when it came to happiness.

CHAPTER
TWENTY-NINE

D evin and Russel reached the reception desk on the hospital's
main floor and asked for the room number for Melody Harpin,
their cat burglar. The elevators were to the right, then left on the fourth
floor. Each man kept to himself, lost in personal thought.

Upon entering the room, they saw Charli and a tall man dressed in
a white coat, stethoscope around his neck, talking.

"Hey, guys. This is the doctor. Chief Charter called and okayed for
him to tell us about Ms. Harpin's condition." She turned to the doctor.
"This is Agent Devin Sonder and Agent Russel Mayer. They are also
working the cases concerning our female." The men shook hands and
the doctor continued.

"As I was telling Agent Avers, Ms. Harpin's brain damage is like
nothing I've ever seen. The brain works on a series of synaptic connections and neuron transmissions."

"Getting close to losing me, Doc," Russel said.

"Sorry." The doctor cleared his throat. "Let's try this. There are lots of
bridges connecting one side of the brain to the other side. In Ms. Harpin's
case, many of her bridges are missing. Destroyed."

"How can that happen?" Charli asked.

"I've seen several things affect the connections: illness, cancer, damage from injury, concussion—"

"Amnesia?" she asked.

"Amnesia is a symptom, not a cause, as such; you get amnesia from a concussion or injury. Another unique situation with the patient is that her frontal lobe is nonfunctional. There's no damage or anything I can see to cause this. It's as if someone went in and zapped her brain in certain places to turn it off. Only the vital functions are operating normally."

Devin saw and smelled Charli's worry. He wrapped an arm around her shoulders and squeezed. "Barry is very different from this lady. He's conscious and thinking. He'll work out his problems, then come back to you."

Charli nodded, rubbing her face along his shirt. It'd be a little wrinkled, but he'd get by. He hoped Marika didn't have to be a messy person. Hopefully what he saw in her home had to do with lack of time and being at the lab long hours. Yeah, he preferred to think that. Anything else would drive him crazy. He liked everything in its place. Hopefully, she could easily adapt.

Devin released his hold on Charli and turned to the doctor. "If I understand correctly, there's little to no chance of her becoming cognizant enough to answer questions."

The doctor frowned. "There is *no* chance of her ever coming back. She is permanently in a vegetative state. If relatives aren't found soon to give advice on her immediate future, then we will have to go to the medical board to get instructions on how to proceed."

Charli sucked in a breath. "Are you saying you're going to kill her? Take her off life support?"

The doctor once again didn't look happy. He probably dealt with this type of issue every day. Life and death was his world. "We're hoping for a living will to give us direction in how the patient wants to be taken care of, Agent Avers. Please be assured, we won't *kill* her." He glanced at his watch. "I have an appointment I need to leave for. If you have any further questions, please e-mail me. You can get my address from the nurse stationed out front." He nodded to each with a smile. "Nice to meet you all."

"Oh, Doctor," Devin called out, stopping the man. "Can we have someone draw blood from Russel here for me to take to the FAWS lab? One of the researchers asked and we haven't had a chance to stop anywhere to have that done."

"Absolutely, I'll have one of the nurses come in here for that. And tell Marika Paters I said hi. We went to medical school together and I haven't seen her for a while."

Devin's panther nearly sprang out of him. Both Charli and Russel grabbed one of his arms and smiled at the doctor. "We sure will tell her, Doctor," Charli said. "Thank you."

With that, the doctor walked out, the door slowly closing behind him. Charli bopped Devin on the head. "Stop that."

He hadn't realized he'd been growling until he stopped.

The three agents stared at the comatose lady lying in the bed. She looked moments from death as it was.

"Well," Devin said, "I don't think we're getting much help from her." He watched Charli take the woman's hand in her own. He'd never seen his fellow agent use her ability. Maybe this was it. After a moment of silence, he said, "What do you see, Charli?"

Her lovely face twisted with sorrow, anguish pouring from her. "Such pain, such sadness. Her cat desperately wants to be released. Can't be trapped in this bodily cage to die so slowly." Tears rolled down Charli's cheeks. "This never should've happened. Never should've been forced together. Unnatural."

Devin thought about Barry and how he hadn't been a shifter when he'd been Perry. Someone was doing this. Someone was making shifters.

"Oh fuck," he whispered. Was this what the mayor and Klamin were doing? If so, how did the pipeline fit in with that?

"What?" Russel asked.

"I was thinking about the mayor and Klamin. Thought maybe Klamin—"

Charli screamed, dropped the cat woman's hand, and nearly collapsed to the floor. Russel caught her and scooped her up, then settled her on a chair in the room.

"What happened, Charli?" Russel asked, squatting in front of her knees. "What did you see?" He dried her tears with his thumb.

"That name you said—Klamin. Her cat freaked out when hearing it. It screamed, 'Kill him, kill him, kill him.' And pain like I've never felt before shot through me. Who is Klamin?"

Devin shared a look with Russel. "We don't know, but he seems to be in the middle of all the mysteries we've got going on," Devin said. The door opened and a technician walked in with a tray filled with needles and paraphernalia. Charli paled and tears formed when she looked at the needle. Devin wasn't sure why.

"I think we're done here, guys. I'm heading home to wait for . . ." She grabbed her purse and hurried out. Russel sat in the chair Charli vacated and rolled up his sleeve.

Devin moved toward the woman in the bed. He felt sad for her. No family. No friends. Nowhere to go. All that because of one person: Klamin. A lot of details floated in his head from the murder scene, the senator's home, the strange wolf, Rupen and Barry, the mayor's phone call, and now their cat woman. And his day wasn't even over yet.

He longed to see and hold his mate for just a moment to revitalize his spirits that had been brought down by the ugliness of the world.

Then it hit him, right in the groin. "Russel, I'll run your blood to the FAWS lab for immediate analysis."

Russel barked out a laugh. "Whatever, man. You just want to bang your mate again." The technician cleared his throat, trying not to show a smile.

Devin lifted his chin. "Well, she's my mate to bang. So there." Both men at the chair laughed. The tech stuck a cotton ball in the crook of Russel's arm, then slapped a Band-Aid over it. He put the vials in a bubble-wrapped package, sealed the top, and handed it to Devin.

"All done, guys. Have a great bang. I mean day." Devin rolled his eyes and took the package from the tech's outstretched hand.

"Yeah, thanks."

Russel worked on getting his sleeve back into place. "Since you're heading south, can you drop me off at the department? I need to visit my mate before it gets too late. Milkan wanted me to get with her. Can't go against the boss man."

"Nope, can't do that. Especially when he tells you to do something you really want to do, huh?" Devin teased.

Russel smiled. "You betcha."

Devin slapped him on the back. "How long do you think you'll be with your lady?"

"I don't know." Russel shrugged. "Could be five minutes before she kicks me out, or an hour if I can handcuff her to something." His grin turned sly.

Devin laughed again. He could never be ready for all the weird things this multishifter would throw at him. "Okay, how 'bout I call you in a little while? I need someone to bounce ideas off and put some order to all the info we got. A beer would be great."

They left the room and headed down the hallway toward the elevator.

"You're on." Russel pushed the elevator button. "I could probably use more than a beer after my meeting."

CHAPTER THIRTY

Marika placed the cold, dead organ on the scale and noted its weight. "Same thing for the heart, Rupen. Noticeably larger than a normal shifter's."

"So that makes what"—Rupen counted on his fingers—"lungs, veins, muscular system, and heart. The essentials for a bigger creature to function at high capacity." He leaned against the counter and pressed his lips into a white line. "The question is why the small brain, and what is the larger wolf for?"

"Technically, that's two questions, sir," Marika said. "But when we find the answer to one, we're probably close to finding the answer to the other."

Rupen picked up the fur pelt piece from the dead wolf's body. "This material is more fascinating than anything else. I've never seen anything like it."

Marika returned to her microscope. "I don't think this skin is natural. It has too many abnormal elements to come about through evolution. It has to be man-made." She adjusted the scope. "What I can't believe is that it's bulletproof. It's so thin."

Rupen poked and prodded the furry patch. "I agree. But look here." Marika looked up. "When I push my fingernail into it, the fur lets it make an indention in the skin." His finger continued to slowly slice through the material, creating a hole. "What the hell?"

Marika's shocked eyes met his. "How can your finger go through, but not a bullet?" She went back to her microscope and jabbed the material with a pick. The tool barely made an imprint. Rupen repeated his actions, creating another puncture.

Marika took his piece and replaced the sample under her scope with it. Again, she stabbed several times, never getting past the top layer. Then she saw something she couldn't believe.

"Oh my god, Rupen. Look." She stepped back and he bent at the waist to look into the eyepiece. "What do you see?"

He was quiet for a moment, then said, "Amazing. It's repairing itself. The jagged edges are melding back together. Could it be the material is self-mending? Even if the animal is dead?"

"Shifters are naturally fast healers, but not this fast," she said. Then a memory came to mind. "Are you familiar with how stem cells work?"

"Not really. Just that organs can be repaired or diseases cured using the umbilical cord. How does that relate to this?"

"Notice how the skin is coming together." She stepped back for him to observe through the lens.

"It's like water rolling onto the beach. Material just flows together, filling in the hole. Is that different than normal?" Rupen asked.

"Very different. Think about it like this." She crossed her arms and leaned against the cabinet. "A shifter's skin heals in layers, one cell at a time. The wolf skin flowed closed completely in seconds."

"Fascinating idea," Rupen said. "Minimizing bleeding would keep the animal alive longer when fighting. How do stem cells relate?"

"That type of cell regenerates body parts. So what if the wolf's blood carried some kind of component that allowed for regrowth?" She could be onto something momentous. Her special research work concerning the creation of shifters hit a snag at this point also. What was she missing?

"Regrowth?" Rupen asked. "Like a new leg grows if one is cut off? Like a lizard that can regrow its tail when it's snapped off?"

"Yes. Exactly. But what triggers the growth? Maybe those shiny things in the wolf's blood have something to do with it. I thought it might be multishifter related, but maybe not. I'm waiting for a blood sample from a multi. Then I'll know."

"But if bullets can't cut through the skin material, what can?"

"Your finger did."

"Yes, we've established that. But how?"

Marika returned to the scope. With the pick, she slowly pressed the material instead of jabbing quickly. The tool slid through with ease. "Holy cornstarch. That's it."

Her boss looked at her with a quirked brow. "What?"

"Haven't you ever played with cornstarch and water?"

"No. What's the significance?" he asked.

She thought for a moment how best to describe a non-Newtonian fluid. She looked around searching for things she needed for this special demonstration. "Take this"—she handed the commander a beaker— "and fill it with water." She pointed toward a cabinet with a sink, then rushed around gathering up an armload of stuff. "Let's go outside."

Rupen followed her to the side of the building where a large garden area was enclosed in a chain-link fence. "What's this all used for?"

Marika unlocked the gate and went inside. "Sometimes we have experiments where we need to see how natural processes act on something. Like how long does it take for fly larvae to grow in a dead body left outside. Cool stuff like that."

Rupen froze midstep. "Are you saying we're walking on decaying bodies?" He looked down at his shoes.

She rolled her eyes. "No, silly. This is where we get ground material for testing in a controlled environment."

Rupen put his foot down. "Thank god."

Marika headed toward the front corner, which looked over the guest parking area. She set a bowl on the ground, then churned up dirt using the metal pick like an ice pick.

"Pour in half the water, please." Rupen followed instructions while she scooped dirt into the bowl. She mixed the water and dirt to create runny mud.

"Okay. You've seen what I've stirred together: dirt and water." He nodded. "Now watch." She slowly dipped her fingers into the mixture and pulled them out dripping with mud. "Moving slowly, my fingers sank into the material. Watch what happens when I quickly stab at it."

She poked several times, fast and hard, at the same muddy water and her finger didn't go deeper than the top of the mud, like she hit solid material.

Rupen's face lit up. "Oh, you're talking about colloidal material. Sure, I know what those are." He proceeded to slowly push his fingers into the mud, then stabbed his finger, only penetrating the very top layer. Very strange material.

Her superhearing picked up footsteps coming from the parking lot. "Looks fun, guys. Can I play too?"

Marika squealed with delight and popped to her feet, then ran through the fence gate to literally jump on her mate. She locked her ankles behind his back and peppered kisses over his face.

Devin smiled. "I like that kind of hello. We'll have to practice that every day."

A sly twinkle entered her eyes. "Yeah, and see how much more welcoming we can be." She felt his cock twitch under her ass. Her body temperature skyrocketed. Suddenly, it was very hot.

"Keep it in your pants, both of you," Rupen said as he gathered the tools from the experiment. "Now get inside before someone sees you and wonders what really goes on inside these windowless walls."

Marika giggled and hopped down. "Yes, back to the lab." She turned to her mate. "Did you ever play with cornstarch and water when you were a kid?"

"Is that where it's hard if you hit it, but soft if dipping slowly?" he asked.

She smiled and kissed him on the cheek. "You are so smart, my love." She noted muddy handprints on Devin's shoulders. "Oops." She looked down at herself to find her lab coat covered with mud. How had that happened? She'd barely touched the stuff. "I need to get a clean coat from my office. Come with me?" she asked Devin.

Rupen rolled his eyes. "No hanky-panky. I want to finish up this wolf and get out of here. It's been a long day."

"Agreed," she said. "We'll be back in a jiffy."

CHAPTER
THIRTY-ONE

Devin smiled at his mate's enthusiasm for life. She always had a smile on her face and a twinkle in her eye. Seemed that way, anyway. Technically, he'd only seen her three times. But each time she was smiling and had that sparkle!

He brushed at the dirt on his shoulders that his mate accidentally put there. If that's what it took to get her legs wrapped around him, then his cleaning bill would go up with no concern on his part.

As he followed Marika to her office, he straightened his jacket and tugged on his shirtsleeves to get them perfectly aligned. Just like his desk and home, everything had its place. He prided himself on the fact that he had mastered the no-clutter, highly organized habits of a good mate. So many other men were slobs, and their mates always complained about picking up after them. His mate would delight in the fact that she'd never have to clean up after him.

In fact, he bet they'd have the cleanest apartment in the building.

Marika opened an office door and flipped up the light switch. Devin stood on the threshold and stared at the catastrophe. Papers were *everywhere*—over the entire floor, desk, chairs, sofa, filing cabinets.

Scientific magazines and books lay scattered on any open spot in the room. He heard his inner panther say, *Uh-oh.*

His mate opened a small closet tucked in the corner. He watched as an avalanche of stuff fell out onto the floor. More books and magazines, a football, cordless drill, hammer, Christmas decorations, and god knew what else. She waded through it like it was nothing and plucked a white lab coat from a hanger.

After sliding it on, she looked at him and smiled. "All ready." His face must've still registered shock because her smile vanished. "What?" Her eyes darted around the room. "Sorry about the chaos. When Rupen came in this morning, I put his ass on the floor and sorta made a mess of everything."

Instantly he felt better. There was a logical reason for the disaster. She was probably very organized like her mother but with working long hours and so much going on, things must have gotten out of hand at home. "Must have been a big battle to make this kind of damage."

"No, not really. My fox and I are super fast. We had him pinned in seconds." Her brow raised. "See, I can take care of myself." She stuck her tongue out at him.

He was on her faster than she thought possible. He had her back against the wall, hands held over her head. "Now, my love. Stick that tongue out once more and see what happens."

That happy spark in her eyes turned to a hungry, lustful look. Fuck, his dick and cat sat straight up to check out what was going on. They both wanted to taste the woman tightly pressed to him. Maybe they had time for a quickie before their boss came nosing around.

Then Rupen's words played in his mind. The man wanted to get out of here, wherever that was. He sighed and ran his lips up her neck. "We need to get back before the head honcho realizes we disobeyed his direct order."

Marika groaned. "Are you always by the book?"

His cat wanted to say no, but the human overruled this time. "Yes. Mostly."

She stretched up on her toes and bit his earlobe. "We have to work on breaking you of that." A coy grin shined up at him. He swore he heard his cock whimper. She took his hand and led him to the lab where the big cheese was bent over a microscope.

"You had three more minutes before I hunted you two down. You could've had a quick quickie."

Devin scrunched his nose. "I'd prefer a bit longer than that." He slid a hand down his mate's backside, taking a handful of plump, perfect ass. She squeaked and jumped forward a bit, keeping her smile for the boss man. Her hand blindly swatted behind her, trying to dislodge his firm hold. Not happening. He changed his mind. He did want the quick quickie. Not happening either.

Then he remembered his excuse for driving down to FAWS. He reached inside his coat chest pocket and pulled out Russel's tube of blood. "Almost forgot to give you this. Russ's blood for multishifters."

Marika plucked it from his fingers and prepared a glass sample for the microscope while Rupen spoke. "The pelt seems to be a colloid with the same attributes as the muddy water. This composite could change the world in many ways. We need to find out who created it."

"That seems to be the mystery of the day for me too. Who is Klamin?"

Both Rupen and Marika spun to face him. "Klamin?" they said together.

Devin smiled. "Guess you two heard of him?" His mate and boss shared a look. His smile turned to a frown. He didn't want anyone sharing anything with her. Even his boss.

"Tell me what you know about this guy." He eyed Rupen for the information.

The lieutenant colonel sighed and looked at the two. He seemed to be deciding on something. "What the hell. This goes no farther than this room. Got it?"

The couple nodded.

"Klamin was contracted with the military in Afghanistan to supervise work on injured soldiers to create—" He stopped. "Well, his work related to decreasing healing time for downed soldiers, among other things."

"Did he succeed?" she asked.

"Don't know. He drove out the gate one night and never returned. We assumed he was killed. Took all the research data with him. His crew said they were at a problem they couldn't get past. The research was halted and the project died as far as I know." He turned to Marika. "What do you know?"

"I've come across his name several times in the files given to me to research the shifter creation theories. But it's in the most recent areas of work, the newer records. Like he added to what the elders started."

"Do you have those files?" Rupen asked. Mari circled the long island to the other side and lifted a box onto the countertop.

"I noticed how different these papers were from older ones. This might be his work." She handed him a thick stack of notes.

"How did he get access to these? They were supposedly found in an unearthed bunker in the Shenandoah Valley not too long ago."

"From what I could understand, he worked in the lab that had all this research. He was able to recreate shifter DNA, then he found something 'miraculous' and his notes stopped there. I followed his research and discovered a flaw in his work. The shifter DNA didn't mix with human blood. The human injected with shifter traits always died, painfully, I'm afraid. His creation theory didn't work."

Devin jumped in with confusion. "Wait. What is the creation theory? And what research do you have?"

Rupen looked at him. "If she tells you about that stuff . . ."

Marika finished his thought. "I'll have to kill you." Both laughed at Devin's incredulous look.

"Seriously?" he said.

"Let me start," Rupen said, "with the beginning, based on what we've deciphered from history and evidence." He turned to Marika. "If something is different from what you've been told, speak up." The lieutenant colonel leaned against a counter. "Around a thousand years ago, a spaceship crash-landed on our planet. Many survived and had no choice but to go on with their lives, here. We assumed their communications capabilities were damaged beyond repair or they would've signaled for help from their planet.

"During their time, they created a species that bridged the gap between animals and humans. We're not sure the reasoning behind doing this, but the fact that they had technology to accomplish this is incredible."

"Wait," Devin said. "How does one create a species? What species?"

Aliens. That didn't shock him. He was a shifter. Nothing shocked him when it came to the paranormal.

Marika raised her hand. Rupen looked at her. "Mari, we're not in school." She snapped her hand down. "Sorry, I can't help but be excited. This is my special project we're talking about. I'm studying the notes and work of these ancient people who crash-landed on Earth. It's unbelievable."

Devin smiled and kissed her temple. "You be as excited as you want. I'll just try to hold on for the ride."

Her cheeks blushed. "Anyway, you create a new species by engineering them. Take the resources available and trial-and-error your way through until you have the traits and characteristics you want."

Rupen nodded. "Yes, and that's exactly what they did when they created the various shifter species on this planet."

Devin stared wide-eyed at them. "That's not possible. I mean . . . you—you just can't mix two living entities together and come out with something new. That's like mixing brownies and cookies to get crownies. It doesn't happen."

Marika kissed his cheek. "Hush. That does work. My first attempt at baking turned out something like that. Mom wouldn't let me touch the oven again."

Rupen continued. "Not too long ago, we discovered a plot intended to harm Earth. With help from others, we were able to find the organizers and take out their compound. Upon interviewing them, we found out about another part of the plot that was developing elsewhere. This may be the other plot.

"This other scheme was far more advanced in its abilities to . . . to take over our country." With their gasps, Rupen held up a hand. "We believe it's actually a conspiracy between Russia and someone inside the States already. If you see or hear the name Yugo Harzoon, let me know immediately. He's dangerous and wealthy, which means he has the capability to do a lot. We're trying to find out who the contact here is and where they are hiding out. This man has the intel we need."

"I've never heard of Yugo Harzoon," Devin said. "I'll get with Milkan and the others to see if they've heard the name."

Marika turned back to the blood sample Devin handed her moments ago. "Hold that thought, Devin. Before you go, Rupen, I want to see what multishifter blood looks like. Do you know much about multishifters, sir?" she asked.

"No," he said. "I haven't had a chance to learn much about the species since there are so few of them. It's quite nice to have one on the fellowship team. We're very fortunate."

"Agreed," Devin said. "Russel is a great guy. I've seen him as a rat and skunk now. He's great at his job, even though bad luck in the form of cats seems to follow him."

"Why a skunk?" his mate asked. "If he sprays himself, he could damage his nose—not to mention our noses—for a week."

Devin didn't want to get into the investigation, so he let the two drift toward the scope and blood plates. Until he had more information, he didn't want to bring up the mayor with the media already converging on their town. He'd let that play out to see if something shook loose.

After Marika and Rupen swapped out sample plates several times and stared through the microscope seemingly forever, they surfaced for air.

"I'll be damned," Rupen said. "The wolf is a multishifter. But the shiny things aren't in the agent's blood. So Perry and the wolf have something none of you born shifters have."

"I saw it too," Marika said. "What do you think it could be?"

Rupen shrugged. "Perhaps you are right about the regrowth theory. But I'll tell you, he didn't find this miraculous healing power without help. It had to have come from something on that alien ship where the original research was discovered."

Devin swallowed hard. How was Charli going to handle it when Mari told her the person she loved was partially alien?

CHAPTER THIRTY-TWO

Devin zipped up the body bag containing the wolf and stuck it in the freezer. He had started his day looking at the dead thing and was ending it the same way. Not ideal in his book. But he was within feet of his mate, with no boss around anymore, so nothing else mattered.

Marika grabbed his hand and headed toward the back of the building. Hopefully they were going someplace other than her office. Wow, that was something else. He wondered if through the years he'd become too rigid, too set in his ways to adapt to the changing world.

The loss of so many lives had taken its toll, hardening him against emotions. The bottom of a bottle had been his favorite sight for far too long.

Now the sight walking in front of him raised his spirits more than anything else ever could. How would he survive if she was lost to him? He couldn't even finish the thought; it hurt so badly. Automatically, he started shutting down his feelings, building that wall that had protected him for months after the double funeral.

His panther swiped at him, telling him to get his head out of his ass. Devin shook his head. No, he couldn't. The loss of his mate would end him. He'd skip the bottle and go straight to the end. Do not pass Go.

Marika pushed on a metal door, taking them outside into a shaded area with tables and chairs. A narrow swath of dirt held colorful flowers and herbs that scented the air. Rosemary and lavender soothed his tortured insides. Until his mate turned and punched him in the arm.

Shit. He shied away, wondering what he'd done now. Scratch that, he knew what he'd done. Doubted himself and her. That was twice she'd left a bruise on him. Maybe she was more capable than he gave her credit for.

"Yeah, that's right," she stated, fists on her hips. "Don't think I didn't smell you freaking out just now. You were all over the board." She sighed and dragged him to a lounge chair in the sun. His mate seated him first, then she snuggled between his legs, wrapping his arms around her. She smelled so good, so soothing.

"Okay, love," she said, "tell me what's going on. Are you regressing to your Neanderthal thoughts?"

Anger crept up in him. "Just because I want to keep you safe doesn't mean I'm a caveman."

"No, it doesn't. It makes you vulnerable to those who want to hurt you and bring you down. It distracts you from your job, which will get you killed." She twisted around and took his face in her hands. "You are correct thinking you can't live without me. But have you thought about how I would live without you? I wouldn't either. Mates can't go on without each other."

He knew how mates worked. What was her point? He didn't want to do what he knew he had to. He had to trust. The last time he trusted his family was safe, they were killed.

"There you go again." She sighed. "What is going through your head? Talk to me, Devin." His cat repeated her sentiment in his head. Were they both against him now?

"Look, Marika. When you've seen what I have for so many years, it gets hard to see the good in the world. Your focus comes to what bad thing is happening next, because there sure as hell will be something bad: murders, shootings, suffering, seeing kids living without food or shelter. It's been drilled into me to not feel. And when I did, I found I couldn't handle it.

"I want you and love you, and I'm trying to find a way to live without being scared shitless you'll be dead when I get home." He squeezed her tightly to him, fighting his fear, fighting the bloody image of his apartment after his cover was blown. No. He couldn't do this.

His defense mechanism kicked in, shutting out all the pain and bringing the cold, hard facts of his latest case to his mind. "Tell me all you discovered today with the wolf. Is there anything to lead us to the second attacker with it?"

His mate sighed. She had to know he was avoiding the subject they needed to talk through. But wasn't that what all guys did?

"Okay, sweetie. I'll let it go for now, but we have to find a solution we can live with together. Got it?" He nodded, thankful she was so understanding. "Rupen and I discovered several things, but we didn't get a chance to put it all into perspective before he left."

He smiled. "I'm very good with perspective, especially when it's not my own." She snorted and rolled her eyes. "So let's hear what you've got."

Marika went through the list of physical traits discovered in the last few hours. Body size larger than normal wolf shifter; respiratory and muscle systems more efficient than normal; skin that was bulletproof, but not finger-poking proof; smaller brain; hard growths on body seemingly protecting areas vulnerable to damage (face and legs); and a multishifter.

"Sounds a whole lot like an engineered superkiller to me. This Klamin dude doesn't seem like a nice guy."

"So you're saying Klamin is responsible for the senator's death?"

He thought about that. "I think Klamin had the senator killed because of a pipeline project."

"The Sea-Sac Pipeline?" she asked.

He looked at her. "What do you know about it?"

"Not much." She shrugged. "Just what's been in the news. An oil company wants to run a pipe from Seattle to Sacramento to expedite oil down to California. It's supposed to make getting oil through the mountains faster. But I haven't heard much about it lately. I think it's been held up for some reason. I wouldn't know why someone would kill the senator over it."

He thought about the phone conversation Russel overheard earlier today. Klamin, Hayseed, and the mayor were in cahoots. Then a comment Russel had said came to mind: the mayor would have more power than he ever imagined.

CHAPTER
THIRTY-THREE

S itting outside behind the FAWS building in a lounger with the hunkiest man alive, Marika was more than exasperated with her mate. Why was this man of hers making things so difficult? She understood his loss and grief. She'd lost family members unexpectedly too. But she didn't let it define her life. Of course, she hadn't been exposed to the underbelly of society as Devin had been.

She was determined to get him through this. Determined to make the sun shine in his life, even if she had to cram it down his throat. She just needed to figure out the best way to do it.

She opened up the picnic basket she'd packed today for her midafternoon snack. Her fox's hyperactivity burned a lot of calories. If she didn't eat a second meal before going home, she'd be nearly dead. And now with her mate here, they could spend the time together.

Plastic containers of fruit, cold chicken, and rolls were stacked on the table next to the lounger they shared. Then she took two water bottles and put them next to the food.

"I made us a snack," she said, hoping he would want to take part. Frankly, she didn't know more than what he'd already told her, and that just wasn't enough. She wanted to know everything about him. After all, he was the man she'd share her life with now. "I figured we could get to know each other a little better."

He nodded and eyed the chicken container. "Ask me anything. I'll always be honest with you."

Oh man. He was so gonna get some later. "So what do you do for fun?"

Devin raised his brows. "I like to organize my clothes."

She giggled and passed him a piece of cold fried chicken. "Not work. I said fun. Like, I like to go on roller coasters."

He made a face like she had lost her mind. "Roller coasters? I guess I like to watch the news."

She blinked and tried again. "What do you do to relax?"

He chewed on the chicken and furrowed his brow. "Hmm. I read."

She sat up, wiggling on his lap. "Reading! I love reading. What kind of stuff do you like to read?"

"Usually my case files," he said casually.

Oh god. It was worse than she thought. "Um, Devin, you do realize that type of reading is not considered relaxing, right?"

He shrugged and swallowed. "I have gone out for a drink with Russel once or twice."

She perked up and grinned. "Oh good! That's really good," she slapped a hand to her chest. Shit, she was starting to worry about him. "What else?"

"I guess the biggest thing is I like to hunt."

A wide smile spread over her lips. "Hunting? In your animal form?"

He nodded. "What other type is there?"

She threw her arms around his neck and kissed his face like this was their first time seeing each other in days. "Thank god!"

"What?" he asked, hugging her tightly to him and kissing her back.

"I love hunting. I'm just happy we could do something we both like together." She gave him a sappy smile and shoved a grape into his mouth. "Eat. I seldom prep meals. A quick sandwich is the most I'll do, so this took lots of effort."

He chuckled and glanced at the containers. "Those have price tags on them. Looks like you picked them up at the deli?"

She nodded. "Yeah, but I hardly ever stop at the deli on my way to work, so this is a great treat today."

"The food is good, so you did a great job selecting what we'd eat."

She blushed under his praise. "Thank you. So how many kits do you want to have?"

He raised a hand to her face and caressed her cheek softly. There was an insane amount of love in his eyes. "Whatever makes you happy is what we'll do."

"Really?" she gasped in complete awe.

"Yes, as long as I am the one in charge of keeping things organized." He pressed his lips to hers when she blew a raspberry. "Don't worry, love. I'll make sure your office is your domain."

"I always wanted a big family, but I have a busy job. Maybe we should just start out with one."

He picked up a grape and rubbed it on her lips. "I agree. We'll learn with the first one and hope we don't traumatize him or her too badly so that we're comfortable having more."

"So what's your favorite dessert?" If he said anything other than chocolate, she might have to reconsider him as her true mate.

"I'm not really into sweets," he said. Her heart took a nosedive toward Heartbreak Hotel. "But I find something chocolatey is always good after a meal."

Yes! He was back on top and she was ready to rip his pants off the way he kept staring at her mouth. "I think you and I will do great."

He gave her another of those scorching kisses she was becoming addicted to. "I know we'll do better than that."

She glanced at her watch and saw it was much later than she'd realized.

"Oh damn," she said, rising from the lounger where she sat with Devin.

He reached out to pull her back down. "What?" She plopped into his lap.

"I have an appointment to meet a guy at a new lab." She felt a vibration through her back where her mate pressed against her.

"A guy?" Devin growled.

Marika rolled her eyes. "Yes, a fellow scientist who needs help setting up his lab or something."

Her mate squeezed her against him. "Let him do it himself. He doesn't need you." She laughed at the jealous pout in his voice. She wiggled around to face him, took his cheeks in her hands, and kissed him, long and hot. Fire scorched her insides. Shit. Maybe that wasn't the best thing to do right now. She just wanted a tease to keep him focused on something else while she went to her meeting. Almost backfired.

When she pulled away, they were both breathing hard. "There will be more of that tonight when I get to your place after the meeting." His smile grew wide.

"Damn right, there will be more of that. How about right now?" Devin leaned in, but she giggled and pushed him back. Her head tilted to the side.

"Someone is watching, my love. It doesn't matter who it is, I'd prefer not to give them too much of a show."

Her mate growled again. He was so adorable when he got all possessive and wanted her to himself and couldn't have her. She had no worries. He'd get all he could handle when they were alone. She intended to have a bite on her shoulder by midnight. He would not walk away from her despite his wimpy reasons. She wouldn't give him the chance. Being mated, she could at least find him easier.

Marika got up from the lounger, gathered all the food into the basket, and held her hand out to her man. He grabbed ahold and she yanked him to his feet effortlessly. He eyed her strangely, still holding her hand. What was going through his head? Did he notice she was stronger than most? He hadn't seen her in her fox form yet. She was saving that for a surprise.

Ever since she was a little kit, watching all the karate movies she could find, she'd wanted to be a Super Fox Ninja. She copied the moves she saw on TV and practiced them in human and fox forms until nearly perfected.

She'd hide in a dark corner, and when her sister or someone walked by, she'd spring through the air making karate-chop motions with her hands, land behind her sister, then karate-chop her more and flip off. She lost count of the times her mom told her to stop flipping off others. She thought that was so funny.

Then taking self-defense classes with Charli had brought back her bouncy spirit after losing it from being exposed to the realities and pressures of school and going out on her own. She hoped to have kits of her own one day who would be interested in some sport or the arts. But for now, she'd save her show for the right time.

Her mate following, Marika stopped at her office to get her purse. She heard papers shuffling and looked up to see Devin gathering loose papers that had been dislodged from the scuffle between her and Rupen this morning.

On his knees, he reached out, dragging more and more to him. From the one page he held, she knew which stack those papers belonged to.

"Those go on the pile behind you that have 'science news' in the footer." Devin collected others and she pointed out the stack for those. Within a couple of minutes, her office was an organized mess. "Wow, Devin. You are wonderful at putting stuff where it goes. I would've gotten to it eventually."

He wrapped a hand around her waist. "Yeah, but I learned something about you just now."

"Oh really? What?"

"Even though the room looks like a tornado may have barreled through it, you knew exactly where everything was. If you wanted something, you would know exactly where to find it. I bet if you had shelves or file cabinets, your office would have carpet showing."

She kissed him. "Of course, silly. I may look disorganized to the untrained eye, but it's my way of hiding all the secret files I have. Would you want to search through all that to see if anything is important?"

"Nope. Not ever," he said. "Good tactic. You're a genius at organized disorganization."

In the parking lot, she kissed him on the cheek and turned toward the employee parking on the side of the building. Except Devin didn't let go of her hand.

She said, "Hon, I want to stay with you as much as you want to stay with me, but—"

Her body jerked sideways when he yanked her in his direction. "Good, I'm going with you. In reality, though, you're going with me since I'm driving."

"Devin—"

"Nope. Don't give me any lip, woman." He smiled as he tugged her to his SUV. "Actually, giving me your lips would be one of the top things on my mind."

Marika tried to pull away. His hand squeezed tighter. They rounded the truck and he opened the door for her. She huffed, "All right, I'll let you come along." And he boosted her onto the high seat.

"Good choice, my love." Devin kissed her cheek, then closed the door and hurried around to the driver's side. He was so sexy. The way his pants clung to his thick thighs when he walked, the way his ass wiggled—nicely rounded ass. His strong hands and forearms. Damn, she had never thought forearms could be sexy. But on her man, they were.

When he slid into the seat, she licked her lips, watching. He took a deep breath and chuckled. "Woman, you will be the death of me." He shook his leg and tried to adjust himself. She laughed.

CHAPTER THIRTY-FOUR

Russel paced outside the city's police department building. He hadn't been this nervous since he lost his virginity, which was in college. Yeah, that was really late for most guys, but nothing about sex was a mystery to him. He knew exactly what it entailed, how to do it several different ways, and the consequences of unprotected sex.

Thanks to all his sisters and female cousins, he didn't need to take Health class in school. He taught it.

Why was he so damn nervous? He knew why. This was for keeps. His mate. His life. If he fucked up and she turned him away, could he handle it? He'd be the first shifter in history whose true mate didn't want him. Fear shot through him. Maybe it was his physical looks she didn't like.

He'd dye his hair whatever she wanted. He'd grow it out or buzz-cut it. He'd never had a shaved head. That could be cool. Of course, he'd insist that she be clean-shaven too. And he didn't mean her beautiful flowing hair.

Oh shit. His cock woke up with the thought of her pussy being slick and smooth. His tongue would slide up to her clit and suck on hot skin. No loose strands stuck in his teeth. That gross thought helped his erection soften. It needed to soften a lot more before he went in. His mate wasn't a shifter, so she couldn't smell his desire. Maybe that was part of the problem.

Devin and Marika smelled what nature had intended for them. No questions for them. They needed to mate and get on with life. The sooner the better for shifter mates.

But damn humans didn't know. They had no sixth-sense radar telling them who was right or wrong. And it seemed with the divorce rate so high, they usually were wrong. He truly believed that in a fifty-fifty bet, there was a 90 percent chance of getting the wrong fifty. His math teacher hadn't appreciated the joke, but hey, life was life.

A police cruiser pulled into a parking spot and a uniformed man stepped out. On his way in the building, he gave Russ a nod, but had a suspicious eye on him. Russel couldn't fault the man. There had been too many police and security personnel murdered for no more reason than a deranged person with a gun wanted target practice.

He pushed those thoughts away. That was hitting too close to home.

He sucked in a breath. All right, do or die. After a step, he thought dying didn't sound that bad. The voice in his head told him to get over himself and go inside. His feet dragged forward, through the front door, up to the officer at the desk. Wow, a desk without bars and bulletproof glass separating it from the public entrance. Another reminder he was in a small town.

"I'm here to talk with Tam—Detective Gibbons." He was going to play this 100 percent business. No teasing or sex talk or asking her on a date. Yes, that's the way to play this. She was professional and very fact-driven. He could do that too.

The female at the desk hung up the phone. "She'll be up in a minute."

He thanked her and stepped away, moving closer to another door. A few people sat in the few rows of chairs on the side of the room. The normal plaques and photos found in most police departments hung on the wall. It may be small, but seemed up to date.

The door behind him opened and he turned. His heart leaped. His mate was at least as beautiful as the last time he saw her. He wanted to pounce, but the voice in his head reminded him about being professional. Now he regretted thinking that. Him, professional?

Detective Gibbons stared at him. Locked eyes and held his gaze. His pulse doubled. Could she not tear her eyes away from him? Was she so enamored with him that she was stupefied seeing him? Struck wordless?

She frowned and raised a brow. "Oh, you." She turned and stepped back into the hallway. Okay, maybe she wasn't stupefied or wordless. But she did take a long look at him. He darted forward and grabbed the knob before the door closed.

His mate was fast. She was already halfway down the hall. He watched her walk. The sway of her rounded hips, narrow waist, and perfect ass. His tongue swiped between his dry lips. *Professional.* Dammit.

He hurried to catch up and followed her into an office. He closed the door behind him, earning him another raised brow. She rounded the corner of her desk. "How can I help you, Agent Mayer?"

Russel sat in the uncomfortable chair in front of her desk and crossed a leg. Then quickly uncrossed it. He wasn't sure if crossing his leg was unmanly, so he kept both feet on the ground. His hands were in his lap—looked like he was playing with himself. He snapped them up to put his elbows on the chair's arms. Shit. Should he steeple his fingers, or clasp them? He remembered reading that the finger steeple was a sign of a smart person. So steeple it was.

"Agent Mayer?"

He looked up from his pointed fingers. "Hmm?" She stared at him with a slight upturn to the corners of her luscious lips. "Oh yeah. Sorry, Detective Gibbons." Yet another raised brow. He wished he knew what that meant—good or bad.

To see her, he needed to look around his arched fingers. Should he clasp his hands now that he'd established his smarts with the steeple?

Maybe cross the leg now? He lifted his leg, then stopped midswing when his left nut squished between his thighs. He tried not to scrunch his face with the slight pain, but he was sure something showed.

"Russel." She said his name, his *first* name. Wasn't that an intimate step or something? He met her look. Her eyes smiled. She was so beautiful. He let out a sigh before he realized he did.

Her cheeks blushed and she turned her eyes to her desk. "Agent May—"

"No," he said, "Russel. Please call me Russel." Again, her cheeks turned rosy. She was so sexy when her innocence showed through.

"Russel"—she paused to smile and he flew to the clouds—"do you want to talk about the armored truck robbery?"

Still floating, he wondered what armored truck—oh, the armored truck—"Yes, the truck robbery. What have you got?"

She rose from her chair and walked to a wall covered in stuff a detective would have on a wall. He'd watched about every police/detective TV show that had ever aired. It started forever ago with *Hill Street Blues* and continued to the newest season of all the HBO series. He had cried when *NYPD Blue* ended. Really. Like a baby.

Russel stood and followed his mate at a distance to—once again—get a look at her.

Professional.

Goddammit. Sometimes he wished his voice was a physical entity so he could beat the shit out of it.

Right, you and whose army?

Shut it.

His mate turned to catch his eyes on her. Her head whipped toward the board. Whoa, her embarrassment was heavy. He shouldn't have been doing that. "Detective Gibbons, I apologize for checking you out."

Idiot human. Don't say 'checking you out.'

"Oh, sorry. I didn't mean to say 'checking you out.' I meant to say 'I apologize for checking you out and getting caught.'" Gibbons busted out in a laugh and his inner voice shook its "head" and walked away. He felt his cheeks warm. OMG, he was blushing. Another first for him. What she did to him . . .

"If we're going to work together, call me Tama," she said, then turned toward the wall covered with photos, drawings, and other stuff.

"Tama. Such a beautiful name." After his mate cleared her throat and looked away, he realized he had said that out loud. His face scrunched in self-anger. "Uh, sorry. I'm trying to be professional. Really, I am. You just . . . just . . ."

Tama crossed her arms and leaned against the wall. "Look, Russel, I'm extremely flattered by your attention and . . ." She waved her hand in the air, indicating everything he'd just done concerning her. "But I'm not the type of person to marry. I spend too much time in the office. My job is dangerous. I'm called at all hours of the night. You'd be better off chasing someone who cooks and cleans and gives you a family."

The smell of sadness reached his nose. Then her gorgeous ass rang. She pulled her mobile from her back pocket. Hmm, he'd never been jealous of a phone before. Tama walked a few steps away to take the call. He turned off his ears to give her privacy. But when she pulled her phone from her ear and held it in front of her, he couldn't help but see her screen.

She scrolled her calendar and stopped on a future date. He saw *Dr. Aveena Schrieffer* on a line next to a time. He turned away as she typed on the line after that. He didn't want to snoop. He didn't like the course of the conversation before the call interrupted them, so he wanted to take it back to the professional level.

When his mate moved toward him, phone call over, he said, "Director Milkan mentioned a few things about the robbery. Mainly that there were human and shifter prints. Any more clues along those lines?"

For just a second, she looked disappointed, but her professional mask came down quickly. "We got fingerprints from the back of the truck right where the dead guard lay, but none of the system's databases are coming up with an ID. Seems this person doesn't exist or he's never had his prints taken. Which is possible, if he's lived on another planet all his life."

Russel knew she was joking, but he just happened to know a certain bear shifter who was MIA. Fuck.

"But other than that," she said, "we just have the crime scene pics." She pointed to a series of photos thumbtacked to the wall. He remembered what Charli and Barry told him and Devin at the hospital last week after Charli and her man were pushed off the road. Barry had transferred the money in a johnboat, and stashed it under a bridge. But there was no evidence of him killing the guard in the back of the truck.

Russel reached out and shook his mate's hand. "Thank you, Tama, for the information. It's helped a great bit." He hurried out of the building. He had a killer to find and a veterinarian to confirm was still alive.

CHAPTER THIRTY-FIVE

At his desk in the fellowship department, Russel's inner voice and brain argued. His voice wanted to stay with their mate, but his brain said his coworker, and a great person, was in danger.

He loved his mate, but she didn't even like him. He did get a smile from her, but he didn't get a good vibe. His heart hurt, knowing how the future looked: lonely.

She mentioned having kids and a family. He wasn't sure he was ready for kids or ever would be after that day of the hostages. If she wanted children, maybe he wasn't the right man for her. Being human, she could love another man, but would always feel something was missing. But for him, he would never love again and probably die of a broken heart sooner than later.

He shoved those thoughts aside. He had to remain positive and believe that Fate knew what she was doing. Focus on his case. And Barry.

He hadn't seen Charli since this morning, nor was she answering her phone. He wanted to believe she was safe, that Barry wouldn't pick this moment to hurt her, if that was his plan.

He dialed Devin and turned in his desk chair, remaining calm.

"Sonder here."

"Hey, you seen Charli lately?" Russel said. He heard Devin ask someone the same question, and a female answered no. Must be his coworker's new mate. A painful ping struck Russel's heart, but he pushed it aside.

"Not since lunch. Why?" Devin asked.

"I was with Tama, talking about the armored truck robbery, and I think we have solid evidence linking Barry to the guard's killing. I had hoped he just carted the money away for Charli's sake, but evidence proves otherwise. He's dangerous, Devin."

He heard "shit" over the phone line. Devin's mate said, "She's not picking up her phone."

"I tried her mobile too, several times," Russel said.

The sweet female voice spoke again. "Do you think Barry is with Klamin?"

"Why would you ask that, Devin's mate?" Russel asked.

"Sorry, man," his coworker said. "Marika Paters, this is Russel Mayer, shifter agent."

"Nice to meet you, Russel," she said.

"You too," he replied, trying to keep despair from the problems with his mate from his voice.

"Here's what we've got so far," Marika started. "The wolf isn't born naturally, but man-made and a multishifter. Barry is also man-made, but only a bear, as far as we know. Klamin is connected to files on creating shifters, so we think Klamin created the wolves and sent them out to kill the senator because of a pipeline project dealing with a lot of money."

"So you're saying since Barry is created, he's with Klamin?" Russel asked. "That makes him that much more dangerous. Shit. I wish Charli would answer her phone."

"Yeah, me too." Devin sighed. "Listen, there's a lot of info we got that we need to sit down and puzzle out. I have a feeling everything we've seen this past week is connected. I just don't know the link yet.

Marika and I are on our way to a quick meeting at a new laboratory on the south side of town. How about we meet you at the bar in forty-five minutes?"

Russel heard Devin and Marika discussing the meeting time. "Okay," Devin continued, "I'll call you in thirty minutes no matter what to update you on our progress."

"Yeah, that'll be good," Russel replied. "I'll wait for the call. T-T-Y-L." He hung up the phone and leaned back in his chair.

Who was this Klamin person? He was responsible for Senator Hayseed's death over a pipeline. That part of the investigation had been solved.

He turned to his computer and wiggled the mouse to kill the screen saver. Into a search engine, he typed the man's name. Three hundred nineteen *thousand* results in .39 seconds. Great. This probably wouldn't help much. But he had time before Devin called him in thirty minutes.

He clicked on the first result. The site read, Klamin—algae extract for women seeking an alternative to hormonal therapy during and after menopause. Oh shit. That wasn't even close. The next several pages were the same. All right, time for a different idea.

Then he remembered the doctor's name he saw on Tama's phone. Was it an invasion of privacy if he googled the doctor? Yes. But she was his mate. He cared for her and needed to know if she was sick or hurt. It was his job to protect her, whether she wanted it or not. That would be a perfect excuse, if caught.

He clicked to return to the search engine and typed the doctor's name. A page popped up showing the pictures of several people and a medical center. He clicked on the female's image with the name Aveena Schrieffer under the photo.

Another web page came up with the female doctor info. He skimmed to the end of the first line of her bio: . . . twenty years as a gynecologic oncologist.

Wasn't an oncologist a cancer doctor?

CHAPTER
THIRTY-SIX

T-T-Y-L?" Devin said. "What the hell does that mean?" He pushed the phone button on his steering wheel to disconnect his hands-free connection.

Marika giggled. "I guess you don't have younger ones around much."

"No," he said, "that I haven't had in a long time." He thought of his little nephew and sighed. A warm hand rested on his arm.

"I'm sorry, Devin," Marika replied. "I didn't mean to bring up bad memories of your family."

He glanced at her with his own expression of apology. "No, Mari. It's not your fault." He turned back to the road. "I need to get past that point in my life. Need to move on." Trying to keep his smell to himself was nearly impossible, especially when most of his worry was for the gorgeous woman sitting next to him. "So what does T-T-Y-L mean?"

"'Talk to you later.'"

His brows raised and he flashed a smile at her. "Seriously? Talk to you later?" He shook his head. "Kids these days will be the worst spellers in history because they don't spell out anything. Not to mention the laziest."

"But think of the time they'd save if they used Morse code."

Devin barked out a laugh. He loved how his mate always had the positive side to see and share.

Marika followed along with the map on her phone as Devin continued to drive them to the laboratory. The area south of town was underdeveloped with square blocks of overgrown weeds. A few rusty warehouses were scattered here and there surrounded by chain-link fencing. The map from the senator's desk came to mind. Especially the one southern section where the pipeline crossed into town limits. He wondered how far that was from here.

Marika's phone said to take a turn at the next street that led up a slight hill. The flat top was covered in broken-up asphalt butted up to a one-floor cinder-block building. He had a bad feeling about this.

"You sure this is the correct address?" he asked.

"According to the map and address, this is it." She looked around. "It is a new business. Maybe they haven't had time to fix up the outside yet."

"Still sorta creepy," he said. "There're no other cars here. Maybe the guy isn't here. What's his name?" Devin parked in front of the main double glass doors.

"Nex is what he said when he called me earlier." A light was on inside, illuminating a reception area. A shadow passed over the desk. "Looks like someone is here. Let's go in." Marika opened her door.

"You go ahead," he said. "I'll try to get Charli on the phone quickly, then I'll be in. You can warn this man your overprotective mate is tagging along. And he has sharp claws."

She leaned toward him across the seat and he met her over the console and kissed her, slowly, with lots of delicious tongue. Too bad they didn't have a little time to jump into the backseat. They pulled apart reluctantly.

"Hold that thought, my love," she mumbled. "As soon as we get back outside, I'm biting you."

He gave her a wink. "Not if I bite you first."

She gave him a sly smile. "You'll have to fight me for it." She ran her tongue over her lips. His body shuddered. That brought a laugh from her. "Wow, I can't believe the very serious, too-tidy investigator lets a few words affect him so much." Marika slid from the seat to the parking lot, blew him a kiss, then closed the SUV door.

He watched her hips sway in her casual dress as she headed for the glass doors. Yup, she would have made him happy. He didn't want to tell her the decision he'd made.

CHAPTER THIRTY-SEVEN

S itting in the parking lot outside the soon-to-be laboratory, Devin sighed as his mate disappeared inside. He pushed the phone button on his steering wheel. After the double beep, he said, "Call Charli Avers." The system's female voice verified the name, then dialed her number. It rang to voice mail. Shit. Maybe it had been a mistake to let Barry, or Perry, go. What Rupen revealed at lunch was enough for him to haul the bear's ass into a cell for safekeeping.

He had a bad feeling that Barry and Klamin were tied somehow. It felt deeper than creator and creature. Barry's involvement in the armored truck robbery was more than just a brainwashed follower committing a crime. There was more to the man. He called Charli one more time with the same results.

Not wanting to leave his mate alone with a strange man too long, he opened the truck door and headed for the building. When he shoved his keys in his pocket, he felt something already in it. He pulled out the wad of napkins that had Russel's blood on it from the café earlier. Damn, he'd forgotten he had that.

Standing close to the main entrance, he didn't want to walk back to the SUV just to toss them on the floor. Instead, he scooped up a handful of pebbles, laid the wad of napkins on the ground next to the door, and covered it with the pebbles to keep it from blowing away. He'd grab it on their way back to the truck. After brushing off his hands, he opened the glass door and stepped inside.

Two things struck him at once: the lobby was vacant, and the smell of the second wolf at the crime scene this morning lingered in the air.

His gun was in his hand before he mentally called for it. His panther pushed at him to find their mate. She was in danger. Had he lost her already? No, he wouldn't think that.

A door was on each side of the desk. He followed the smell to the far side. Throwing the door open, he waited a beat before he ducked and hurried in, gun ready. Inside, he flattened against the wall, watching and listening.

His panther's eyesight took over, scanning the dark space. Before him, a large area was filled with cubicle desks that looked as if they hadn't been used in years. On a couple of desks, huge boxy computer monitors sat next to old CPU towers. Those things were from the 1990s.

A noise came from the opposite side of the room. He snaked around the low metal walls separating one desk from another. He debated whether to call out to Marika. He didn't want to give away his position, but desperately needed to hear her voice, hear she was alive.

As he slid closer to the back of the room, another smell reached him. A strange scent that was familiar. He sniffed. Yes, he'd smelled it recently, but where? He reached the end of the aisle bisecting the room. That smell—where had he come across it? He prepared to jump into the back passageway. Then he saw the top part of . . . an elevator? He hadn't heard a ding, so hopefully his mate was just around the corner.

His panther lending him strength, he sprang into the back aisle. At that second, the answer to where he'd smelled the strange scent hit him. It was the moment at the morgue when the body bag was unzipped with the dead wolf inside.

Before his feet touched down from his leap, two wolves tackled him, slamming him to the floor. "Devin! Run—" Marika's voice registered in his brain. He rolled toward the sound to see a tall, bulky man with one hand over her mouth, the other around her waist.

By the expression on her red face, his little mate was pissed. He watched as she mashed her heel into the foot of her captor. She then drove her elbow into his gut, bending him over. Turning in his loose hold, she faced him and shoved a knee into his crotch. The wolves growled, reminding him he had his own adversaries.

He rolled, bringing up his gun. He fired shots, hitting each wolf in the chest with no damage done. "No bullets, Devin. Remember the cornstarch and water." The moment at her lab a few hours ago flashed in his head. The skin was a colloid. Only slow finger jabs got through the material. So what was he supposed to do now? Poke them to death? Not likely.

Both shifters squared up with him still on the floor. They reared back on their haunches, ready to spring and tear the shit out of him. He didn't have time to fully shift. He threw his arm in front of his face in time to feel hot breath, but no teeth.

As he looked up, a cute little fox fumbling in a dress body-slammed into one of the wolves, taking out the other in the process. They tumbled into the cubicles, knocking down several. Immediately he shifted to his panther. His clothes restricted his movements from an awkward fit, but his claws and teeth worked fine.

One of the wolves climbed to its feet quickly, going after his foxy lady. Before he could respond, she ran directly at the wall. What the hell? Was her eyesight gone? Inches from the wall, she sprang straight up, then pushed off with her back legs. She flipped back, over the wolf behind her, as the creature slammed into the drywall, its snout busting through the panel.

Upon landing on four paws, she dived for the trapped wolf's neck. She latched onto the skin and slowly, as slowly as one could go in the heat of a death-defying battle, closed her jaw. Her teeth sank in farther and farther as the wolf thrashed its body trying to shake her off. Seconds later the wolf went still, its throat torn from its body.

Standing, watching, his panther's mouth fell open and his butt hit the ground. Who knew? His mate was a freaking killer ninja. Fuck. Could she do that in bed?

He heard bones breaking and tendons stretching. The remaining wolf shifted into a bear. Oh fuck, multishifter.

Devin pushed to his feet and stepped back, but the bear was faster than a normal bear shifter. The monster scooped up his cat and threw him into the cubicles, sending him crashing against the end of a row, starting a domino of falling walls, burying the cat under debris.

From under collapsed desks and computer parts, Devin's panther slinked out, looking for his mate. Hearing a roar from the bear, he snapped his head that way and saw his fox dangling between the bear's back legs, jaws locked on its groin. The massive animal stood helpless, unable to reach its rear feet with its paws, unable to step on her between its legs. The only option it had was to sit, squishing her.

The thought must've come to the bear because it positioned to fall back. Again, Devin found his cat diving through the air before he issued a command. They made a great team. He agreed with his cat that if a fox can take down two wolves, then a big-ass cat could push down a bear. At least, he hoped, or his love would be a sexy flat fox.

As Marika did earlier, Devin body-slammed the massive animal, knocking it sideways as it sat back on its hind legs. His mate wiggled away, but her dress was snagged on the bear's claw. Having no hands, she wasn't able to simply unhook the material.

Devin scurried to help his mate. They had to get to the front of the room to escape. He heard a ding from the wall and the elevator doors slid open. Before the doors fully opened, a sting hit his shoulder. A dart with a fuzzy red tail was sticking out of him. An identical shaft was embedded in his mate as his vision narrowed to black.

CHAPTER THIRTY-EIGHT

Marika rolled onto her side and reached for her pillow. It must've fallen off the bed. Her hand banged into hard metal. Her eyes popped open. This didn't smell like her bedroom, or Devin's. The metal her fingers hit were steel bars of a large jail-like cell. She slowly sat up, trying to keep her head from spinning.

She lay on a green cot against a concrete wall. The air was cool and damp, a bit of mustiness coming now and then. The rest of the small room had two more holding cells and a desk and chair by a door several feet away.

Swinging her feet over the side, they hit something solid. She looked down to find her mate lying on the floor, either sleeping or unconscious. Then the fight in the lab came rushing into her head. She and her mate were tranqed and brought here. Who in the hell would have reason to kidnap her and Devin?

The concrete was cold on her feet as she sat next to Devin, cradling his head in her lap. "Come on, baby. Wake up for me." Her fingers brushed hair from his forehead. A moan vibrated in his throat. "That's it, sweetie. Come back to me." His lids opened and his beautiful eyes looked up at her. So soulful, so deep. "Hey, there you are."

He sat up and lifted a hand to his head. Marika warned, "Careful, you'll be dizzy for a few seconds. But then you'll be okay."

"Where are we?" he asked.

"Besides a jail cell, I can't say."

"What?" His head lifted and he looked around. Then he whipped around and ran his hands all over her. "Are you injured? Anything broken or bleeding? Do you have any pain?"

She smiled at his concern for her. "I'm fine, love. Calm down." She grabbed his hands, holding them tightly to her chest. "We're okay. Sit next to me and let's figure out what's going on."

The crazed panic left his eyes and his frantic expression melted away. "You sure you're okay?" She brushed her fingers over his cheek.

"Yes. I'm perfectly fine." He wrapped his arm around her and moved her onto his lap where he held her to him. She burrowed her face against his chest and took a deep breath. A calmness washed through her that she hadn't known she needed.

The door at the front of the room opened. The man she knew as Nex, the man who had dragged her into the room of cubicles, entered. Her eyes narrowed at him.

"You creep bastard. Why are we locked up? We didn't do anything to you. We don't even know you," she called out.

He knelt in front of the cell door and scooted a tray loaded with food through a slot at the base of the door.

"No, you don't know me. But we know you, Ms. Paters. We have plans for you, an offer you can't refuse."

She snorted. "I can refuse a lot, asshole."

He replied with a smile. "Will you refuse your mate's life?" Devin's arms squeezed her to him. She kept her mouth closed. The man stood.

"Both of you sit quietly. The boss is busy for several hours, and I'm not babysitting two weak shifters. This is enough food and drink to hold you until tomorrow, if need be." His dark eyes focused on her. "It's nice to meet you, Ms. Paters. With your assistance, I'm sure we'll be even stronger. Unstoppable maybe." He left the room.

Marika chewed on her lip. "What do you think he meant?"

"Whatever it was, it wasn't good. You heard them; they have plans for you. They will take you away from me." His arms tightened until she could hardly breathe.

"Devin," she complained.

He loosened his hold. "Sorry, my love."

She didn't know what to say. Everything looked rather dim at the moment. Devin tapped her leg. "Up you go, love." He pushed her to her feet, then got to his own. His fingers started unbuttoning his rumpled shirt and sleeves. She liked this, but wondered what was going on. Him shifting wouldn't help them get out, as far as she could see, anyway.

He untucked his open shirt, but left it on. His heated eyes met hers. Breath caught in her throat. He took her into his arms and twirled her around the space. He smelled so good, and her face rested on his molded chest.

She looked up at him. "What's going through your mind, sweetie?"

His grin turned devilish. "I've changed my mind about mating with you."

Marika pulled away from him. "What? Changed your mind?"

He nodded. "Yes. I'd decided to keep you safe by not mating with you. Even though you are stronger and ninja-like."

Anger flared inside her—

"I said I *had* decided. Now I've changed my mind," he said quickly.

"Oh." A smile came to her face. Then she realized what he meant to do. "Oh," she said in a raspy voice. "Here? Now?"

Hungry eyes looked at her. "He said it would be hours before anyone would check in on us."

"Yeah, but . . . here?" she asked, her eyes taking in the sparse room. "What if someone is watching?"

"I already checked all around us. Doesn't seem to have cameras."

He dipped down and lined kisses across her neck. She tipped her head back with a soft moan. "Okay, here it is, then."

Their clothes came off in a rush and she tried not to think of anyone else watching them at the moment. He wanted to mate with her now and she wouldn't refuse. She needed that link, that connection to him to feel more at peace. And if they died, well, they'd die together. On second thought, fuck that! No way in hell she'd let anyone lay a hand on her man.

He kissed her and pulled her back into the heat of the moment. She sucked on his tongue, nipping at his lips and moving down to his jaw. He stroked her with his hands up and down her back, raising goose bumps on her sensitive skin. They moved by the bars, and she pushed him against them, the glazed look of need in his eyes driving her actions.

She wouldn't be deterred by his touch. She wanted to give her man all the pleasure she could. Kissing her way down his rock-hard abs, she continued down until she was kneeling in front of him. With a hand curled around his hot, smooth length, she glanced up.

His jaw was clenched and harsh breaths made his chest rise and fall. "Sweetheart, you don't have to—"

She grinned and licked him from root to tip. He groaned and she did it again.

"I want to." She flicked her tongue over his shaft, putting the head of his cock into her mouth. She gripped him harder and slid him farther down her throat. He groaned and drove his fingers into her hair, holding her head hostage and guiding her movements.

He didn't thrust hard, instead he groaned and encouraged her as she took more of him into her mouth.

"Ah, baby. Your mouth is so hot."

She suctioned her cheeks tight and flattened her tongue, widening the back of her throat to take him as far as possible. Then he pulled back, his cock leaving her lips coated in her saliva.

"That's the sexiest fucking thing I've seen all day."

She loved how his animal made his voice raspy and knew his control was near shattering. Another suck and he moaned, his hips flexing forward slightly. She continued sucking him deeply and releasing him slowly. Once she had him tensing, she increased her speed and gripped his left ass cheek with one hand while fondling his balls with the other. She jerked, squeezed, and sucked harder every few seconds, making him grunt and hip thrust.

"You've been holding out on me, love," he mumbled. "I didn't realize how amazing you were with those beautiful lips of yours."

An increase in pressure made him press his back farther into the bars and repeat the thrusts into her mouth. She wanted him to come. She felt his body tensing, muscles locking into place.

She knew just what to do to make him go over the edge. She sucked harder, flicking her tongue under his dick, allowing her spit to dribble down the sides of her mouth and using it to continue jerking him faster. When his body started shaking, she raked her fingers-turned-to-claws over his ass and scratched him deep, letting him feel the bite of pain as he closed in on his climax.

He tried to pull her head away from his cock, but she took him deeper and sucked faster. He came in her mouth, shooting streams of hot cum down her throat.

"Fuck!"

She swallowed and jerked him, taking everything he gave her.

"God, baby," he said through choppy breaths as he helped her stand. The animal sat just below his skin, ready to come out at any moment. His eyes shone bright gold and his voice was barely understandable.

She licked her lips and grinned. "You taste good."

"Fuck, sweetheart." He flipped them around so she was the one with her back toward the bars. "Don't say shit like that."

She grinned. "Why not? It's true."

He kissed her with a renewed desperation that she liked in him. She wound her arms around his neck and raked her nails over the back of his neck. Somehow, knowing that this man who loved to be in control and have everything in its place lost his cool because of her was sexier than anything.

He pressed his body to hers, his hands gripping her hips. She curled her legs around his naked waist, glad he held her up between his body and the bars. The broad head of his slick, hard cock slipped into her and surged forward.

Their gazes held as he filled her. He went in fast and hard, until he was deep inside her, his balls pressed snugly against her pussy.

She dug her fingers into his shoulders, her claws scratching at his skin, leaving thin, bloodied lines. "Give it to me, Devin."

He brought his head forward and licked up the side of her neck. "I'm going to give you everything you want, baby."

"Good. Fuck me harder."

He pulled back and surged into her with increased speed and power. Every drive pushed her into the bars. She gulped, trying to get rid of the dry throat from breathing harshly through her mouth.

"More," she mumbled.

He continued to ram her with his cock, the feel of him inside her making her fox wild and desperate for more. She was so close. Her muscles tensed at the nearing climax.

"I fucking love being inside you," he whispered by her ear, biting down on her jaw. "When we get out of here, I'm taking you outside and fucking you in the open forest."

She groaned and closed her eyes, visualizing them doing just that. "Open? Why?"

"I want to watch you under the moonlight. My dick sliding in and out of your wetness. I'll pull it out of your pussy slick with your heat and shove it in your mouth."

She inhaled sharply, her body getting hotter the more he spoke. "Oh god."

"I want you to suck your own juices off my cock. Then I'll press you up against a tree, like I have you right now, and shove my dick deep inside you. Leave your knees shaking and my cum dripping down your legs."

She cracked. A soft scream left her throat as tension turned to a wave of pleasure that made her feel like she was floating. He didn't stop driving into her like a madman. He continued, harder, faster, until his cock pulsed inside her and he tensed. He growled by her ear.

"You're mine, mate. I'm keeping you."

He bit down on her shoulder, hard, embedding his canines into her flesh. Shock held her immobile. Shock and the fact that she couldn't move. He filled her channel with the heat of his cum, his teeth still embedded in her shoulder. Semen spurted from him with every short thrust until he wasn't moving any longer, his cock still deep in her sex.

A rush of emotions from both of them filled her chest. She couldn't make heads or tails of all the affection she felt coming from him. Much to her shock, her heart dropped all walls and an instant wave of love and care for Devin filled her heart.

She wasn't sure what was going on. Was this what mating was? This immediate sense of belonging together? This open love and devotion that they shared? And she was sure he felt it too. There was a new link between them once he bit her. A love so powerful, so strong, she was a little scared by it.

Maybe she'd never been in love or even lust before, but this was so new, so different, she was going to need time to adjust. Not that her fox cared or even her heart over her brain. She loved Devin, and it was decided that she and her fox were keeping him. *Mine.*

She couldn't argue with her fox, but she hoped the more she got to know him, the easier it would be to deal with all this love and affection that came out of nowhere.

He kissed her bitten shoulder and licked at her already scarred wound. "I'm going to fuck you all over again, right now."

She nodded, a smile working her lips. "This time, I get to bite."

CHAPTER
THIRTY-NINE

Devin snuggled with his mate. He had honestly thought this day might never come. He'd searched and traveled whenever he could, always looking for the one. Granted, her office looked like a tornado went through it, and she had a tendency to make a mess. But she was funny, loving, brilliant, and *his*.

And now, no matter where she was, he would be able to find her. Their bond, their link, not only tied them physically, but soulfully. He felt her presence as she felt his. Following this invisible pull would lead them to each other, always. Only one thing could sever that bind.

His mate rolled in his arms to face him. "You know, I might be able to squeeze through the slot at the bottom of the door in my fox form."

He glanced at the opening, then her. "You think? It's really narrow."

"And I'm a secret foxy ninja." She wiggled her hips against him.

He couldn't help the smile on his face. "Yes, you are definitely foxy. And quite limber, I might add." Her blush made her so adorable. She morphed into her animal, then hopped to the front of the cell.

He watched as she lay on her back, stretched her front paws under the top bar of the slot, and pulled herself through until the bridge of her nose hit the bar. Her snout was the only thing keeping her from sliding all the way through.

She pulled and shoved, inching her head farther out, tilting it down for the bar to go over her snout. Devin felt pain on his nose and back of the neck. He knew it came through their connection and his mate. She put herself in agony to try to save them. God, he loved her.

The pain grew to make his eyes water. He slipped to the floor, needing and begging for a way to take her pain. If her body was limber enough, her head would continue to tilt forward, as her body moved under the bar, driving her snout against her chest. A whimper escaped her locked jaw.

"Stop, my love. You're hurting yourself. Stop," he cried. The pressure on his face felt as if it would pulverize his nose into his brain. He had to do something to help her. Save her from this.

He straddled her slight animal form, wrapped his hands around her ribcage, and shoved her under the bar. A line of fire seared down his face, but his hands were on the other side of the cage. A strip of skin was missing from the top of his mate's snout, but she was through.

She shifted to her human form, rubbing her nose, and gestured for her clothes. Devin didn't move. His eyes roamed her body. His hand reached through the bars, headed toward her neatly trimmed triangle of hair.

Suppressing a giggle, she slapped his hand away. "Stop that. We have to get out of here. Get my clothes, horny toad." Devin licked his lips, but did as she said and slid her clothes to the other side of the cell. She dressed quickly, then pulled the keys from the table by the door.

After freeing her love, they poked their heads out the door to see what there was to see. Not much. Concrete walls, floors, and ceilings as far as the eye could see. They really were in a prison. But Marika knew from the damp air and slight mustiness that they were underground.

She looked at him. "Which way, love?"

Devin's brows pulled down. "One way looks just as bad as the other. You choose."

Marika stepped into the hall, sprang into the air, and whirled in circles. When she landed, she faced to the right. "This way."

With a smile, Devin asked, "What was that stunt all about?"

"That?" she said. "Oh, that's nothing. Just my version of heads or tails." Devin shook his head, hiding his smile with his hand.

"What have I gotten myself into?" he asked.

Marika smiled back at him. "A whole lotta fun, mister." She grabbed his hand and they hurried down the hall, hoping to find an exit sooner than later. They'd be out of there in no time.

CHAPTER FORTY

After driving around for hours, Charli walked into her house, physically and emotionally exhausted. Her worst nightmare had come true. Barry had left her. He remembered his life and realized he had better elsewhere. Someone he loved more.

She was cried out. Numb. Based on what Rupen had said at lunch about Perry, maybe it was better that he was gone. But she couldn't see him as a mean person, someone who would purposely hurt others. Perry, perhaps. Barry, never.

After dropping her purse onto the table—leaving her unanswered phone inside—she trudged toward the bedroom. She wanted to curl under the covers and never come out. What would be the purpose? There'd be no reason, would there?

She turned a corner and standing in the hall outside the living room, Barry looked at her. She couldn't read his expression. Was he happy, sad, angry? He didn't move toward her or away. No words made their way to her mouth. Nothing escaped the sludge in her brain. Was he here to say good-bye? Yes, that must be it. She turned away from him, unable and unwilling to face reality.

That put him in motion. "No, Charli, don't walk away from me. I can't handle that." He stopped her with a hand on her shoulder and gathered her into his arms. Charli had just thought she was cried out.

But tears, fresh and hot, rolled down her cheeks. She couldn't handle this either. He held her tightly and she wrapped her arms around him. They stood for a long moment until he kissed the top of her head.

He asked, "Do you believe I love you?"

"I don't know what to believe. You said you did, yet you ran from me." She pulled away from him. "You said the man you were before was dead." Anger built with each word. "You said it didn't matter who that person was. He no longer existed. But you bolted the first chance you got."

He tried to pull her to him, but she refused to let him. "Charli, I love you more than life itself. And if you knew Perry, you'd be shocked it came from my mouth."

"Then why did you leave me? We can work this out. I'm sure Rupen understands the situation and knows you're not like that anymore."

"Am I, Charli?" She stared with tear-ridden eyes into his. Her heart said he wasn't, but what did she know about the real him? "I am ashamed and horrified of what Perry has done with the past five years of his life. He wasn't totally to blame. He was under mind control . . ."

She looked stricken. "Mind control? What are you talking—"

"Nothing," he lied. "Don't worry about it. I've got it covered. Perry's been saved by a beautiful angel he'll do anything to protect, who he'll love for the rest of his life. I asked you a question over the weekend and did a piss-poor job doing it. Now, I'll do it right."

He shoved his hand into his pocket and knelt on one knee. From his pocket, he pulled a small diamond ring. Charli's heart stopped along with her breathing.

"It's not nearly big enough to match your beauty or how much I love you, but we'll deal with that later. But Charli Avers, will you marry me, eventually?"

Her brain was jammed with questions, yet empty of words. Did this mean he was staying, that he would never leave her again? Yes, that had to be what he meant. She had to ask: "So you learned about your horrible life and ran from me to go ring shopping?"

"Well, I had some other things going on, but yeah. I'm getting my priorities straight, and you top the list in several ways."

"What do you mean 'several ways'?"

He looked at her for a second. "Do these questions mean yes, or no, about marrying me?"

She chewed on her lip. "I don't know. I'm debating how long I want you on your knees groveling."

He dropped his chin to his chest to hide his grin, which was unsuccessful. "As long as you want me to, baby." She stepped up to him, took his face in her hands, and brushed a kiss over his lips.

"Yes, Barry. I will marry you, eventually. Promise me you'll never leave me again."

He returned her kiss harder. "I will never be far from you. I go where you go." He slipped the ring onto her finger, then carried her to the bedroom. Their lovemaking was slow and deliberate. So different from before with the raunchy words and domineering personalities. But it was still as intense. His hands and hot mouth over every inch of her skin. Soft caresses down her curves and flesh. Lips and tongue sucking and lashing her tender spots.

Her orgasms were much more powerful with her body slowly brought to peak, once, twice, three times before he allowed her to go over the edge. Stars exploded behind her closed lids, and a sharp pain on her shoulder sent fire straight to her pussy, bringing her around again. He pounded into her one last time, then she felt hot liquid fill her insides. Barry collapsed on top of her, his weight deliciously pinning her to the bed as she drifted into sleep.

Sometime during the night, Charli reached out for her love. The bed was empty except for a piece of paper her hand came across. She whirled up and snapped on the bedside lamp. The note trembled in her hands.

Charli,

There is something I must do. I can't tell you about it because the less you know, the safer you are.

I told you I'd never be far from you and I'm not. I love you too much to go anywhere without you by my side. I have something to finish that never should have been started. I'm sorry I can't elaborate. I do this to protect you to my last breath.

I will be back. Soon. Believe that. Believe in me. In us. I will return to you very soon. Believe me, Charli. That is all I am asking you. You said you'd marry me and I'm holding you to that. No takebacks.

I love you more than life.

Barry

She believed in him. She loved Barry too much to think he'd leave her, knew him too well to doubt him. In her heart, she was absolutely positive his words were truthful. He'd return to her soon.

CHAPTER FORTY-ONE

Klamin closed the mind link with the plant shifters in the fellowship's office and sat back in his leather office chair. The plant on Agent Mayer's desk told him that the two detectives had talked on the phone and had discovered Klamin's name and his role in the senator's death. And it seemed Ms. Paters and her mate Sonder were on their way to meet Nex. Finally something was going as planned.

He rose from behind his desk and paced the suffocating office. He would either kill Sonder or keep him in exchange for Paters's cooperation. Either way, neither were seeing the light of day again. The fellowship would come down, one agent at a time, if need be.

Then he didn't know what to do with that bastard dickhead Harzoon. The Russian was more of a pain in the ass than he was worth. If Klamin didn't need the dickwad to get black-market items, then the little shit would've been gone a long time ago.

He had to get his master plan rolling before that happened.

He stormed out of the office to the elevator and slammed the up arrow button. He was glad he had made the elevators in this place extra speedy. He hated to wait when he had stuff to do. Hell, he hated waiting even when he didn't.

Finally out in the late afternoon air, he took a deep breath. Sometimes being cooped up under tons of concrete and dirt sucked the life right outta him. Soon he wouldn't have to hide anymore. He would sell every drop of water, every mineral and metal, and every human in this country. He would quietly take over each city and run it into the ground, make as much money as he could, and find the next place to exploit.

He was creating the perfect shifter species. He had taken the knowledge from those who came here before him, those who long ago created the first species of shifters to protect Earth, and had evolved it into a higher being. A creature able to do things only told in legends and stories. And he would control it.

It would bend to his will like papier-mâché to its mold. He would have the power to control everyone and everything around him. Then those who wronged him would curse their ancestors' names for their actions.

Klamin took a deep breath and shook off the anger. He was starting to sound like a psychotic, pussy-whining human. He laughed out loud, listening to the sound echo through the valley.

In the distance, across the valley floor, he saw a human form walking. The swagger and sway looked familiar. Could it be? He really needed to update his own body with shifter abilities. To see for a mile and hear ants on the ground would add greatly to his survival, on the planet and off. Perhaps Ms. Paters would lend him a hand with that. After he put her under his mind control, of course.

He watched the form in the distance run in his direction. Fast. Faster than any human could possibly move. The closer the person came, the surer Klamin became, until the man stood before him.

He gave the man a quick hug and slap on the back.

"Welcome home, Perry."

ACKNOWLEDGMENTS

This book wouldn't be possible without some amazing people supporting me.

My readers. Thank you for having my back in everything I write and always loving my work.

Tina Winograd. Your continued support and knowledge of all things is amazing. I can't thank you enough for all you do.

Mr. T (aka Hubby). Thank you for pushing me and believing I can rule the world. One day, I just might.

My kids. Aiden, for your love and random (only when you want) hugs. Alan, for sitting with me while I write, to keep me focused (it mostly worked). Angie, for the cute emoji messages (I love the little whale). You can be anything. I know; I'm proof of that.

Julie. For your unwavering support and willingness to read anything I send you. No matter how bad it looks.

My Curvy Girls and Street Team. Thank you all for your support and telling everyone about my books. It's massively appreciated!

ABOUT THE AUTHOR

Milly Taiden is the *New York Times* and *USA Today* bestselling author of numerous series, including the Paranormal Dating Agency, the Sassy Mates books, and the Federal Paranormal Unit novels. Milly loves writing sexy stories so hot they sizzle your e-reader. When her curvy humans meet their furry alphas, inhibitions give way to animal instincts—and carnal desire.

Milly lives in Florida with her husband, children, and spunky dogs, Needy Speedy and Stormy. She is addicted to shoes, Dunkin' Donuts, and chocolate and is aware she's bossy. Visit her online at www.millytaiden.com.